# WITCHES, PRINCESSES, AND WOMEN AT ARMS

# WITCHES, PRINCESSES, AND WOMEN AT ARMS

## EROTIC LESBIAN FAIRY TALES

EDITED BY
SACCHI GREEN

## CLEiS
PRESS

Published in the United States by Cleis Press, an imprint of Start Midnight, LLC, 101 Hudson Street, 37th Floor, Suite 3705, Jersey City, NJ 07302.

Printed in the United States.
Cover design: Scott Idleman/Blink
Cover photographs: iStock
Text design: Frank Wiedemann
First Edition.
10 9 8 7 6 5 4 3 2 1

Trade paper ISBN: 978-1-62778-228-9
E-book ISBN: 978-1-62778-229-6

# Contents

# INTRODUCTION

How often have you tried to envision "he" as "she" when you're reading fairy tales? Those flights of imagination can sweep you up into worlds of magic and sensual delights—or would, if only so many heroes winning the day (and, of course, the girl) didn't get in the way. Don't you long for heroines who win each other?

I certainly do, so in this anthology I wanted erotic romance and wild adventure with women who use their wits and/or weapons and come together in a blaze of passion. The wonderful writers showcased here gave me all I hoped for, and even more. Some adapted traditional tales, and some updated old stories to contemporary times, not merely changing the gender of a character but making the female aspect essential. Some created original plots with a fairy-tale sensibility, while some wrote with merely a subtle aura of fantasy. Their heroines are witches and princesses, brave, resourceful women of all walks of life, and even a troll and a dryad. There are curses and spells, battles and intrigue, elements of magic and explorations of universal themes, and, yes, sex, sensuality, and true love, all bound skill-fully together into complex and many-layered stories.

Royalty or a miller's daughter, a woman warrior passing as a man, a sorceress in flowing robes, even a window inspector dangling in harness on a high-rise building—who better to rescue a long-haired captive in a tower?—all of them are made so real that you long to touch them, and be touched. The relationships are intense, sometimes quick to ignite, sometimes all the hotter for restraint that flares at last into a fierce blaze.

In all my years of editing anthologies, I've never read so many submissions that were beautifully written and just what I'd asked for. And I've never had so much trouble choosing which to use to fill the finite space in this book. I can only hope that readers will get as much pleasure from these stories as I did, and that *Witches, Princesses, and Women at Arms* turns out to be, to quote a certain beloved film with a unique take on fantasy traditions, exactly, "As you wish."

Sacchi Green
Western Massachusetts

# STEEL

## Cara Patterson

The citadel fell when the princess was fourteen.

The guardians claimed it was impregnable, but no one warned them that their enemy was armed with a dragon. Princess Sianna and her mother fled through the catacombs of the city, leaving the bones and ashes of a king behind.

Some of their people escaped with them, but they scattered to the four winds. It was safer, her mother said. Talbot, the man who had burned her father, was a commoner and would never be accepted as king unless he had a royal bride. He knew the princess still lived, and he would be hunting her, Mother said.

It felt like cowardice to hide, moving from village to village, unknown, often unwelcome, yet they had no choice. Until they could find a champion, Mother said it must be so.

Mother told her they would return to claim what was theirs one day. They would return. Even when Mother started smiling at a smith in one of the towns. Even when they stopped running, and found a small house to call their own. Even when Mother and the smith were hand-fasted, and her belly grew round with another child.

Sianna—no longer called Princess—smiled for her mother, but with every merchant who passed through the town, they heard stories from the west, from the lands that had once been theirs. The kingdom revolted against the tyrant, but Talbot was merciless. His dragon scoured the fields of those who opposed him, burning crops and people both.

"We will return," her mother assured her, one child, two children, three children later. "When the time is right."

The time, Sianna was coming to understand, would never be right.

Her mother would quietly wait out Talbot's death, surrounded by children who were not of royal blood, and who would never know what it was to be hunted as a prize for a murderous bastard. Her mother could stopper her ears against the news from the lands that had once been theirs, the deaths, the violence, the cruelty.

Sianna still had nightmares of the victims of the dragon. When they had fled through the tunnels beneath the citadel, she had pressed her hands tight over her ears, stumbling after her mother in the darkness. She had tried to muffle the sound, but there were too many people, too many screams.

Maybe her mother had those dreams too, but she drowned them out with the wails of newborns. She wanted to forget, but Sianna knew she herself never could, not as long as people who had been her friends, her family, were dying in the flames.

Sometimes, her mother spoke of marriage, but Sianna cared nothing for it. Instead, she worked in the smithy with the man who was not her father. He taught her the nature of metal, and how to bend it to her will. While her mother grew plump and soft, she grew hard, steel tempered in the flames of her true home.

When another convoy came, this one from the citadel itself,

demanding payment for Talbot's mercy, Sianna knew that the time had come. They had fled, but their past would follow them to the ends of the earth, and she had no intention of running anymore.

While her mother wept and wailed to her husband in their small house, her infants sniffling around her skirts, Sianna went into the smithy. There were blades there built for her hand. She was not tall, but she was broad, strong, and the weight of the sword in her grip was right. She armed herself and slipped away into the night, garbed in clothes stolen from the smith.

Her warm brown skin betrayed her origins, and it was known that Talbot hunted a woman of those lands, so in the shadow of the forest she hacked her hair short, and bound her breasts beneath the mail and leather she wore. None would glance at a surly squire with a short mat of black hair and shoulders thick with muscle.

She knew she had no hope of reclaiming the citadel from Talbot, not as long as the dragon lived, but there were sorcerers and mages who could enchant a blade, and make it strong enough to kill a dragon. That was what she would seek.

She followed whispers and legends and rumors.

If Talbot's men crossed her path, she fought them. Her battles were clumsy at first, but by and by, she learned. She blooded her blade. She strengthened her sword arm. She smiled quietly in the darkness of taverns as people spoke of the brave knight with no sigil who stood against the tyrant.

Talbot's men were everywhere, though many of them were not seeking the lost royals.

She had no doubt they sought the same thing as she did.

If some enemy could learn how to slay a dragon, then Talbot's advantage would be gone. What he did not think on was the fact that she could follow his men, find where they hunted, see who they sought, and when they set a pyre for a witch—save her.

Three soldiers were little enough challenge, the rest of their legion still bent on subduing the village.

She cut them down, and hacked through the bonds pinioning the witch.

The witch stared at her, bruised and shaken, but defiant. "I am not your prize," she said through bloodied teeth and lips.

Sianna smiled mildly. "No," she agreed, "but you will come with me."

The witch had no strength to fight, beaten as she had been. Sianna lifted her up onto her own gelding, Tar, mounting up behind her, and galloped away. There were shouts from other soldiers, who gave chase. Sianna cursed through clenched teeth, spurring her horse onward.

"You're a witch," she snarled at the woman before her. "Do something."

The witch laughed, the sound racked with pain. "Save you so you can make use of me?" she whispered. "I think not. No man commands me."

Sianna was in no mood for words. Instead, she snared the witch's hand and thrust it between her thighs, then returned her grip to the reins. The horse was flagging, weighed down by two, and the countryside was wild, the terrain treacherous.

The witch jerked her hand back. She was staring. Sianna could feel her eyes boring into her face. Tar leapt beneath them, over a fallen tree, and the witch grabbed at Sianna, holding tightly with one arm. Her other hand extended toward the sky, burns from the rope visible on her pale skin, while her fingers twisted and curled as if snatching dust motes from the air.

Clouds poured together, thick and black, and thunder cracked. Blades of lightning cut down from the heavens, catching on nearby trees. Sianna's horse screamed in terror, picking up speed, and behind them, the burning trees fell, blocking their pursuers.

Sianna's heart was racing.

She'd heard rumors of how powerful some witches could be. It was said they were element weavers, spinning the elements as some would spin thread. But to manipulate the weather so easily, and bend it to her will? Suddenly, armor and a sword and shoulders as solid as steel meant nothing.

The witch sagged against her arm and Sianna had to transfer the reins to one hand, to hold the woman with her other arm. She did not know if the woman was playing her false or truly exhausted, nor did she care while the soldiers still hunted them.

She knew the mountains well enough to find a cavern before the horse collapsed with exhaustion. The rain was still pouring down outside, and the damp blackness of the cave was a welcome respite. Tar's hooves clattered on loose stone, and he refused to go farther.

Sianna swung down from the saddle. The witch all but fell down with her, folding in her grip. True exhaustion, then, Sianna thought grimly. She looked around as her eyes grew accustomed to the dim light. The cave seemed endless, stretching into darkness, but the floor was bare but for loose rocks. She hoisted the witch over her shoulder, carried her to the smoothest part of the floor, and set her down with as much gentleness as she could. It was a long time since she had needed to be soft-handed.

Her leather cloak had kept her dry, but the same could not be said for the witch, soaked to the bone and shivering. Sianna crouched on her toes by the woman, studying her, then rose and went to Tar. She withdrew her only other coarse, homespun shirt and breeches from the pack.

The witch was still as Sianna stripped her bare and dried her chalk-pale skin, avoiding the bruises the soldiers had left behind. She cleaned what blood there was, then dressed the witch in the clothes.

It would do no good, she thought, as she draped her cloak over the woman, if the first witch she found died in her care.

Tar whickered impatiently.

Sianna smiled at him. He had done her well, and he knew it. She returned to him, removing the saddle and her packs, setting them on the ground. There was a rag to wipe him down, and he knocked his muzzle against her shoulder.

"No sweet treats tonight, I'm afraid," she murmured, running her fingers from his brow to his muzzle. "But the next town we reach, you shall have all the carrots you care for and as much sugar as I can carry."

In the quiet, broken only by the faint, rasping breaths of the witch, the patter of the rain outside, and the occasional crack of thunder, Sianna fed and settled the horse and set about lighting a small fire. It was unwise, but it was cold, and chilblains made her hands ache.

There was little dry wood to be had. Leaves and twigs had been blown into the cave, and served well enough as kindling. Sianna huddled by the small fire, longing for the heat of the forge. She winced, uncurling her fingers over the flame, the heat easing the bone-sharp pain.

The change in pitch of the witch's breathing made her raise her eyes from the fire.

The witch was watching her, catlike, wary. Her eyes were golden, Sianna noticed. Like honey in sunlight. She was not young, but she was younger than Sianna first assumed, her stature small, almost frail. Her hair was also deceptive, a sheet of silver-gray, straight as a blade.

"Why?"

Sianna looked back down at her hands. They were swollen already, and she rubbed them together. "Why what?"

"Save me?"

Sianna raised her eyes to her. "I think you suspect."

The golden eyes closed. "They believe I have the power to subdue their would-be king."

"Do you?"

The witch's mouth turned up at the corners, delicate lines creasing her features. "I take no part in the petty wars of men."

"That doesn't answer the question."

"No," the witch agreed quietly. "It does not. But neither did you." She opened her eyes, and pushed herself up on one arm. "Tell me."

Sianna rested her hands on her knees, watching the flames. "I saw the citadel burn, the day Talbot took the kingdom and killed the king," she said finally. "I heard the screams of the people. I was driven from my home, and now, he's driving others from their homes too." She looked up at the witch. "My mother and I lived in fear, running, knowing he would not stop until he cowed everyone. And he won't, unless someone stops him." She was silent for a moment. "I thought you might be able—willing—to help me."

"For the glory of victory?" The witch said mockingly. "To be the savior of the kingdom?"

Sianna looked at her in contempt. "So no one else has to live as I have." She prodded the flames with a stick. "No one should spend their lives running, afraid that they might be killed or raped or worse." She snapped the stick, tossing it into the flames. "A king's first duty is to protect his people. Talbot is no king." She looked back down at the fire. "He is no man of any worth."

The witch laughed, a soft, musical sound. "On that matter, we are agreed."

Sianna rubbed her right hand with her left, trying to ease the lingering ache. "Now you," she said. "Answer my question."

"Do I have the power to defeat a single man? You saw what I can do, child."

"You can manipulate the elements," Sianna agreed, "but the elements aren't men."

There was a flicker of approval in the golden eyes. "Indeed." With effort, the witch sat up, drawing Sianna's cloak around her. "And defeating a single man is not enough, when his armies are rooted now. You can cut the head off a viper, but that hardly helps when he's only the largest viper in a nest."

Sianna looked down at her hands. They felt large, clumsy, useless. "I used to think it would be simple: my blade, his heart, and slaying his dragon, and all would be well."

"His dragon?"

There was something in the witch's tone that made her look up. "The dragon that burned the citadel. His weapon."

The witch shook her head. "No. No weapon. Weapons do not live." Her fingers curled around the edge of the cloak and she stared into the fire. "Better call the poor beast what it is: a slave. No dragon would willingly serve a human master. They—like those blessed with magic—have no interest in the squabbles of men."

"Then why does this one?"

The witch only shrugged, watching the flames.

Sianna remembered hearing the bellow of the dragon as it soared overhead. It was huge, the color of rust and hot iron. They said that Talbot rode it himself. They said that he was the first to be accepted by the terrifying creatures. It was said—by those who knew nothing of magical beasts—that he had tamed it.

"We free it," she said.

The witch raised her eyes, startled. "What?"

"The dragon," Sianna replied. "You say it's a slave. How is that any different from the cruelty he's inflicting on the people of the kingdom? If we free the dragon, he loses his greatest weapon, and then maybe the people will be able to fight themselves. A nest of vipers is easier to destroy with no fire-breather to protect it."

"Free the dragon," the witch murmured, shaking her head.

"It would burn you alive as soon as let a human approach it."

"Talbot approaches it," Sianna said quietly. "If it's a slave, as you say, then he'll have safeguards in place. If he can approach, then other people must be able to as well. All I need to do is set it free."

"And if it kills you, once you free it?" The witch was staring at her.

Sianna shrugged, the leather of her jerkin creaking softly. "If it's free, it can't be used by Talbot," she said. "The kingdom won't be cowed by dragon fire anymore, and they'll fight back." She smiled briefly. "Whether I live or die is hardly relevant."

The witch shook her head. "You're a madwoman."

Sianna couldn't help laughing. She couldn't remember the last time she had truly laughed. It was far too long ago. "Perhaps," she agreed. She looked across the fire at the witch. "I know you take no part in the affairs of men, but maybe you would be willing to help me free a captive dragon?"

The flames were reflected, dancing, in the witch's eyes. "How can you know you can trust me? You don't even have my name."

"And I won't ask for it," Sianna said. "I know the power a name holds. You can give me your name if you want to, but now, I only ask for your help." She hesitated, then added quietly, "You can call me Sia."

The witch rose. She walked lightly, as if barely touching the ground. She circled the flames to kneel at Sianna's side. Her fingertips touched Sianna's cheek, and she searched Sianna's face with those golden eyes. Sianna looked away self-consciously. Few people paid attention to her, and fewer still looked at her so intently.

The witch's lips touched her brow, as soft and cool as her fingertips, then each cheek, then lastly, Sianna's lips. Sianna's breath caught, and for a moment, her lips parted, before she pulled back, flushed, mortified, confused.

"You have my protection," the witch whispered, lifting her hand. Her fingertips echoed the touch of her lips, light as air, and Sianna swallowed hard. "I am yours to lead."

Sianna's hands were clenched around the edge of her tunic, and she nodded, looking down, then swallowed again. The words seemed to be fighting to get out. "We should get some rest," she finally said. "We can start planning tomorrow."

"When I'm not being burned at the stake," the witch agreed, rising. Her fingertips grazed Sianna's cheek again, and Sianna felt gooseflesh rise the length of her body, a delightful shiver running through her. "Will you rest with me? It will be warmer. You are cold."

"W...with you?"

Golden eyes glinted by the firelight. "I don't bite," she murmured.

In hindsight, it was the worst night's sleep Sianna had ever had.

That was saying a lot for someone who had spent her life on the run, and had slept in hedges, and under carts and a thousand other cold and hard places that did not have a warm, slender witch's body curled against hers.

It was not something that had troubled her before, but then, no one—woman or man—had looked at her as the witch did: as if she were worth looking at. She knew she was not what anyone would consider beautiful. She was too broad, too muscular, too strong. Yet the witch had looked at her and touched her lips to Sianna's.

By the time the witch woke, Sianna had been up for hours. She had tried to sleep, but when the witch shifted against her and small breasts brushed against hers—unbound for the first time in days—the sensation was unbearable.

She could nod and smile, though, and pretend that she was only thinking of the dragon and the citadel.

They left the cave that day. The storm had cleared, and the sun was warm.

"Your doing?" Sianna said dryly.

The witch only smiled.

They were several days from the citadel, but with some grass and oats, Tar seemed in fine spirits to carry them both. The witch rode behind Sianna, her arms around Sianna's waist, her thighs framing Sianna's. Sianna tightened her hands on the reins, drew steadying breaths, and tried to focus on her plans.

It became easier the closer they got to the citadel.

Every town and village they passed bore the scars of Talbot and the dragon. Seared bodies rotted on gibbets. People took their coin, asked no questions, and kept their eyes down. It was painful to see it. Her mother's fear had been bad enough, but here, in the shadow of the citadel, people were broken.

By night they took shelter in ruined houses, and the witch held Sianna as old nightmares flared anew. More than once, she woke, a scream caught in her throat. More than once, the witch held her, soothed her, stroked her brow, and once, just once, she had done so much more than kiss her until her head felt light and all nightmares were forgotten for a time. That was the night they were beneath the walls of the citadel, where the roars of the captive dragon could be heard echoing in the canyon that curved around the city like a wall.

All plans were forgotten at the sound.

Sianna felt frozen to the bone, a thousand memories smothering her: the blackness of the passages beneath the city, the smell of roasting flesh, the taste of bile and vomit in her mouth, bloodstains everywhere and the screams. Gods, the screams.

She was pulled back to herself by warm, insistent lips on hers. The warmth seemed to spread from them, and she drew a breath. The parting of her lips was wordless invitation, and the witch deepened the kiss, her tongue darting against Sianna's own.

Sianna could not recall much else beyond the witch's lips that night, or the silken feel of the witch's silvery hair slipping through her fingers. She tasted of sweetwine and mint leaves, and left Sianna's lips soft and bruised.

Their lantern had burned low, but in the moonlight, the witch's silver hair shone. Slender fingers undid tunic and mail. The strips of cloth binding Sianna's chest unwound and soft, gentle hands caressed the aching skin, earning a whimper from Sianna.

When the witch's lips touched her breast, Sianna forgot any shame or blushes, and when the witch's hand stroked across her backside, she drew the witch's mouth back to hers. It was only a diversion, she knew, but by the Gods, it was most welcome.

The witch's hand slid beneath the waistband of her breeches, and Sianna stifled a sharp whimper as the witch's fingers teased along the folds of her sex. She touched as if she'd touched Sianna a hundred times before, her eyes on Sianna's face as one finger slid into her body, thrusting slowly, the heel of her hand grinding at the tight, hot, throbbing knot at the top of her sex.

Sianna fell back on her elbows, her breath coming faster when the witch lowered her head, silken hair sliding along the tingling expanse of Sianna's lined chest, and a catlike tongue darted over each nipple, then warm and cool breath washed over them in turn. Her skin was prickled with gooseflesh, and when the witch suckled on her breast, she could not stop one hand from moving to hold her there, teeth and tongue teasing a nipple that had been crushed and was aching with sensitivity.

Her hips moved of their own will, grinding against the witch's fingers, while her other hand kneaded at the witch's back.

She had no voice, no words but small, panting gasps as fingers thrust within her. The press of the witch's hand, the heat of her palm, the warmth of her lips made Sianna's head spin with giddiness, while eddies of pleasure washed through her. It rose like a tide, and she arched her back, keening into the night when the witch buried her fingers deep, until all was still and shivering silence.

They should have lain still then, but the witch's mouth was on hers, claiming her shivering gasps. She couldn't recall which of them pulled the witch's dress off, but like her hair, the witch nearly glowed in the moonlight, as pale and slim as Sianna was broad and dark, and they lay down together in the tangles of the blanket and the cloak.

When they were spent and quiet, Sianna slept better than she had in days, her dark head resting upon the witch's breast, flesh to flesh, safe and close. The witch's fingers curled in her hair, and for a moment, Sianna knew peace.

It was but a night. When dawn came, it was put aside, a pleasure and indulgence to be kept for later.

There were whispers in the towns they had passed that Talbot intended to unleash his dragon again soon. If they were going to liberate it, it had to be immediately, and before anyone could suspect that two women were hell-bent on bringing down the tyrant. If they did suspect, Sianna thought wryly, they would probably laugh themselves sick. Women always were underestimated.

The plan was simple.

Everyone who had the misfortune of visiting the citadel, or living in it after its fall, could point visitors to the dragon's pit. The amphitheater was once where the citizens gathered to celebrate or watch performances. Now, the roof had been torn apart and replaced with iron grids that folded together to seal the beast in.

Brave visitors could dare a peek through the bars, and that was exactly what Sianna and her companion did.

The dragon was bigger than Sianna remembered. She felt sick with terror at the sight of it. The witch's slim hand slipped into hers, and squeezed her calloused fingers in wordless support. Sianna took a steadying breath and nodded, forcing herself to search for some clue as to how the dragon was restrained.

"Spikes," she whispered to the witch, as they shared a bowl of soup in a tavern not far from the amphitheater. "There are metal spikes hooked into its jaw."

The witch looked ill. "Iron?"

"Most like."

"No wonder it stays." The witch pushed the bowl away from her. "Iron weakens all creatures of magic. They love gold, but hate iron."

Sianna stared at her. "That's a weak dragon?"

"Small, too," the witch said quietly.

Sianna's hands were shaking. She didn't notice when they'd started shaking, but they trembled so much she had to put her cup down. The witch's hand covered hers, but she couldn't meet the witch's eyes.

"I can free it," the witch said softly. "Your intentions are good, but you need not face it."

Sianna looked up at her. "I have to," she whispered, her voice breaking. "There are guards there, and soldiers, and I won't have you getting killed for my damned stupid idea." She lifted the witch's hand, kissing the back of her fingers. "You've kept us unnoticed, but I need you there to open the gates."

A furrow creased the witch's brow, but she nodded. "Come," she said quietly, drawing Sianna by the hand, and leading her up to the small room they had taken above the tavern.

On the narrow bed, she unrolled a strip of cloth, and lifted out a gold pendant on a braided strand of silk. She wrapped her hands around it, closing her eyes, and murmured words in a language Sianna could not understand. When her palms opened, the pendant was glowing, as if red hot. The witch lifted the silk, and laid it around Sianna's neck.

"A protection," she whispered, pressing the pendant to Sianna's chest. She rose on her toes, and her lips met Sianna's. It was a soft kiss, chaste, but drew a shiver from Sianna nonetheless.

"Another protection?" she asked faintly.

The witch smiled, her fingertips to Sianna's lips. "Only a kiss," she murmured. She looked to the window. "The guards change just before dawn. Are you ready?"

Sianna hesitated, then pulled the witch closer, kissing her for perhaps the last time. She could feel the witch's smile against her lips. "As I'll ever be," she whispered.

They exchanged a final kiss, then Sianna took up her sword, and made her way out into the fading night.

The citadel was quiet, and Sianna knew it well enough to make her way down to the gates of the amphitheater. That was where the guards saw her. The witch had hidden them as much as possible, but no one could be truly invisible.

There were more soldiers than they expected, and when she heard laughter as the seventh man knocked the blade from her hand, she knew why. Someone had betrayed her. The only person who had known was the witch.

She sagged back against the barred doors, panting, her mouth metallic with blood, as a man dressed in his finery emerged from the shadows. He was some years older than her, and handsome in a gaunt way.

"Boy's his father's double, isn't he?" he said to one of the guards. "No wonder he was recognized. No one mentioned the old man had any bastards."

"Not acknowledged ones," the guard replied. "We only knew about the princess."

"A secret prince, then." The man smiled. It didn't reach his eyes. "Come of age and ready for vengeance on me, no doubt. Positively mythical."

"Talbot," Sianna whispered.

"So you've heard of me, then?" Talbot laughed quietly. "You have your father's idiotic notion of heroism, boy. Come to slay my dragon, have you?"

She stared at him. He was just a man, but he was the one who had taken everything from her. "Yes," she whispered. "To slay your dragon."

He walked a little closer, but stayed out of arm's reach. "Your father tried that," he said. "He melted like butter in the sun. It was quite impressive." He glanced through the gridded metal gate, then back at Sianna. "I don't suppose you want to tell me where your sister is?"

Sianna smiled at him. "No."

For a split-second, fury blazed in his eyes, then he laughed again. "Oh, well," he said. He snapped his fingers and the remaining guards dragged Sianna to her feet. "If you're so keen to fight my dragon, do try. It's a little hungry, and I'm lacking in entertainment." He picked up her sword, as she was shoved through the narrow gateway toward the pit. "Do try to last a little longer than your father, hmm?"

Her sword landed in the blood-darkened sand at her feet, and the gates slammed closed.

The place reeked of sulphur and blood and rotting flesh.

Behind her, Sianna could hear the long, low rumble of a dragon's breath. Gods, she felt sick to her stomach. Her sword was at her feet, and she could pick it up, arm herself, but the witch's words came back to her: they love gold, but hate iron.

Her trembling hand reached for the pendant at her neck.

The witch was right when she said it was her protection.

She turned, freezing in fright at the sight of the dragon. It was so close, so big, its teeth as long as her forearm. But it hadn't attacked.

Sianna stared up at it, holding its eyes, and removed her gauntlets and mail. The metal clattered and sang as it fell. She finally drew the necklace from her neck, the small disk of gold dangling from her hand.

The dragon's nostrils flared, and the massive head moved closer to her.

She kicked aside the armor and approached, her feet making no sound on the sand. "A gift," she whispered.

Her heart almost stopped when the huge face came down to her level. The dragon sniffed at the gold, such a meager token, but without hesitation, Sianna bound the cord around one of the horns on its nose.

"For you," she said, her hands shaking so much she could barely draw the knot tight.

A thunderous rumble in the dragon's throat made her jump back, but the dragon remained where it was, slowly turning its head, revealing the spike sunk in behind the ruff of its neck. There was dried blood around it. Sianna stared at it, then ran back to the gate, snatching up her sword and shielding it in its sheath.

Her step-father would have killed her for using a sword as a crowbar, but it worked. The spike pulled free in a mess of thick blood. She heard cursing, heard Talbot shouting, and ran to the dragon's other side, levering the other spike out.

She heard the whistle of an arrow, and heard the scream of the witch from above a moment before she felt the thump of the bolt into her back.

"Oh," she said blankly, falling against the dragon's neck.

The dragon raised its head, sending a blast of fire toward the gate.

Above them, metal was screaming, and dewy daylight poured in through the grid that had been torn apart like paper. The dragon bellowed, snatching Sianna up in its talons and leaping, its wings spreading, as it burst up and out into daylight.

Sianna could see the world rushing around her, her head light. She could feel throbbing where the arrow was imbedded in her back. "Down," she whispered. The witch was down there, somewhere. The witch could help.

But the dragon was free now. Why would it stay? Could it even understand?

She didn't know, and the world was fading around her. She heard cries, and before the blackness took her, hands on her face, and then only silence.

The scent of sandalwood was the first thing that came back to her. Sandalwood and warm wax and honey. She was lying—on her belly—in a tangle of sheets, on a bed that felt soft as feather down, and there was no pain in her back.

She opened her eyes, squinting, buttery daylight filtering through pale curtains that she recognized. Her chest felt tight as she pushed herself up onto her forearms, looking around. The royal bedchamber. It looked as it had before. Talbot must have appreciated its rare beauty.

Something moved behind her and she sat up, turning sharply, reaching for a weapon that was not there. Nor was her clothing. She was bare, but for the sheets around her hips.

The witch was sitting beside the bed. She looked pale and tired, as if she hadn't slept, but she was smiling, and Sianna reached out to her.

"You healed me?"

The witch's fingers tangled with hers. "A little."

Sianna threaded their fingers together. "The dragon?"

The witch smiled slightly. "He and I may have...quieted Talbot and his supporters," she murmured, tracing her fingertips along the back of Sianna's hand. "A witch and a freed angry dragon who knows those who harmed him? They cast down their arms in seconds." She nodded to a broad balcony beyond the windows. A coiled pile of red and gold scales lay there, slumbering in the sun. "He guards you now, and Talbot awaits justice in the dungeon."

"I thought you didn't interfere in the affairs of men?"

Gold eyes met hers. "We did not interfere in the affairs of any man."

Sianna's heart fluttered strangely in her chest. "For me?"

The witch's lips touched their joined fingers. "My name is Falon," she said quietly. Mischief lit in her eyes. "And I have a mind to have you here, in the would-be king's bed."

Sianna tugged on her hand, drawing her onto the bed beside her. "This isn't the would-be king's bed," she said, looking around the room that should have been hers. "This is the queen's bed."

"We had best hope the missing heir remains missing," Falon murmured, tracing her fingers along Sianna's belly. "I doubt she would want to know about us getting up to mischief in her bed."

Sianna chuckled. "Too late for that," she said. "You've already got into her bed once."

Falon sat up, staring at her. "You?"

Sianna sat up too, pushing her fingers through her hair. "According to the records," she said self-consciously. She looked at Falon. "I didn't lie to you. I just..."

Falon silenced her with a kiss. "You didn't know if I was trustworthy," she murmured. "So you're her Highness, Princess Sianna?"

"I was," Sianna agreed, coiling a strand of Falon's hair around her finger. "Perhaps, I can learn how to be again." She kissed Falon again, lightly, then drew back with a quiet sigh. "But first, I need to help my people."

Falon smiled. "You have an advantage over your enemies," she said, one hand pushing the sheets aside. "You have a dragon who considers you a friend, and a witch who will interfere in the affairs of a queen."

Sianna looked down as Falon's hand moved lower, her breath catching when fingertips teased her. "I can see that," she said, though she had to smile. She caught Falon's hand, holding it against her thigh. "You'll stay?"

Falon's smile was brilliant. She leaned close, and whispered against Sianna's lips, "You have my protection."

Sianna's fingers combed through Falon's hair, and she kissed her again. "I hoped you would say that."

# ROBBER GIRL

## Madeleine Shade

The last raven left when the weight of winter forced the golden carriage deep into the snow. I had spent most of my journey north to the Snow Queen's realm on foot, so the ride was a welcome change—one I wasn't eager to give up. The men sent to guard me were cursing about the stuck wheels when the sound of swords rang out. I stayed hidden inside, hoping the screams belonged to raiders even though I knew it was a foolish hope. When rough hands pulled me out of the carriage, I kept my mouth shut and my hands tucked away in a fur muff given to me by the prince and princess. The band of thieves could have the gold, for all I cared. Like it or not, it was time to move on. Certainly, I could hitch another ride on my journey north.

"See ya later, boys," I said, waving the brigands aside. After all, I'd seen worse—much worse.

A hand slapped me across the mouth, stilling my repartee. "You're not going anywhere." I dropped the fur to the blood-soaked snow.

The remains of my escorts lay scattered across the snow-covered slopes curving up from the frozen road. A grizzled old woman advanced toward me.

"Let her go," she said, licking her lips. "This tasty morsel belongs to me."

My captor released me so suddenly that I fell forward on my knees in a snowdrift. All around me, the band of thieves bowed to the robber queen. She reached down, yanked her curved knife from the ribs of a dead guard, and raised the blade to tickle my throat. *Sorry,* I thought, *I won't be able to find you after all.*

I closed my eyes against the image, waiting for the death-blow, but it never came. The blade fell away from the tender skin of my neck and a hair-raising scream forced my eyes open. A lithe girl rode the old woman's back, yanking her wiry gray braids like reins.

"Curse you, you devil's spawn," the robber queen cried out.

Not a single one in her band of thieves moved to help her.

"You should have kept your legs closed then," the girl gloated.

The robber queen fell to her knees. "Have mercy on me, child."

Yet the girl refused to release her hold. "Promise me the prisoner first and then I'll let you go."

The robber queen attempted to nod, but the girl's hold on her braids was too tight.

"Yes, yes," the old woman brayed, "anything for my precious darling."

The robber girl released her hold on the grizzled braids and leapt nimbly off her mother's back. She stomped through the crushed snow and stepped on a dead guard's bloody back to get a better look at me. Even with her human stepstool and black thigh-high boots, she had to look up at me. I'm used to being taller than everyone else. It comes from a shady family history. No black sheep, but my great-grandmother had a thing for the color red and its allure to werewolves. What can I say?

The robber girl smiled, a feral grin that made my nipples stand involuntarily erect. *What sharp teeth you have*, I thought. Suddenly, I wished I had brought my great-grandmother's red cloak along for my journey, even though it's not my favorite color; I look best in a green so dark it appears black in dim light.

Up close the girl appeared to be around my own age. She watched me with deep-blue eyes. Her blonde hair spread about her fair face like a halo. Her pink lips puckered as she looked me over from head to foot. In that instant, I hated my inherited darkness—my black eyes and dark hair, dusky skin and plum-colored nipples. More than anything, I wanted to be all cream and strawberries and gold like her.

The robber girl finished her appraisal and placed her small hands on either side of my face. She pulled me down to her, pale fingers wound through the thick cloud of my loose hair, and kissed my lips, tugging on them with her sharp little teeth. My pussy quivered and clenched as she probed my mouth, tonguing each tooth before she released me.

"Don't worry," she said, patting my cheeks as though I were a child. "You're safe now."

*Safe from what?*

The robber girl grabbed my hand in hers and pulled me past her proud mother and the ring of thieves to a reindeer tied to a towering pine tree.

"I suppose you expect me to carry both of you," the reindeer lamented.

I've never liked talking animals—too many bad memories—so I looked up to study the perfection of the cloudless blue expanse stretching above me.

There was a smack, a hand against flesh, and the muscles of my ass clenched even though I was left untouched.

"Knock it off, Bae," the robber girl said. "You are plenty strong enough to carry both of us."

I wanted to lift my skirts, kneel at the girl's feet, and feel her small hand heat the flesh of my round ass. *Spank me,* I thought. *Ride me,* I thought. And then I blushed furiously. *What has come over me?* I questioned myself. *Too much travel,* I told myself. *I've been alone too long.*

"Come on," the robber girl said as she tugged at my hand.

The reindeer—*Bae,* I reminded myself—knelt in the snow.

I moved to mount the shaggy beast, but I must not have moved fast enough because the robber girl's hands pressed against the firm flesh of my ass. I pushed back. *Yes,* I thought.

She smacked my asscheek hard enough that I could feel it even through the padding of my heavy skirts. Everything else seemed so surreal, I relished the sting. It made everything clearer.

"Let's go," she said, abrupt.

I shrank inside myself at her censure and swung my leg over the reindeer's bony back. She mounted behind me, pressed tight against me, and placed my hands on the reindeer's harness. "Hold this, girl," she commanded.

"My name's Gerda," I said.

"Good," she said. "You can speak after all."

"I'm looking for someone."

The robber girl chuckled and drove her heels into the reindeer's flanks. "Take the long way home, Bae."

The reindeer lurched to his feet, and I tightened my hold on the harness.

Her cool little fingers slipped under my blouse and began to play the hollows of my ribs. She pressed closer, rubbing her tits on my back. The heat between her thighs pressed into me. I couldn't help myself, I began grinding against the reindeer's back.

"You're a naughty one, Gerda," the robber girl said as her hands pushed up higher to flick my nipples.

*Yes.* I moaned. *Don't stop.*

The robber girl kneaded my tender flesh, teasing my full breasts with clever fingers. My juices were filling my panties as my rocking became more frantic.

"Faster, Bae," she shouted. The reindeer raced through the trees. My head dropped back and she bit my neck and pinched my nipples hard between her fingers. The orgasm ripped through my body, every part of me shuddering from the release.

"That's a good girl," she said. "We're going to be such good friends."

The robber girl smoothed my flesh and tugged down my blouse. I slumped forward, embarrassed by my wanton behavior.

Evergreen trees thinned as we entered a high mountain valley, dotted with wooden structures. Bae stopped at the largest building, a rustic barn with a high loft. Next to it sat a log cabin with a steady stream of smoke curling out of the chimney. The girl leapt off the reindeer's back and opened one of the barn doors, leading Bae into the welcoming warmth. She peered up at me, looking as innocent as a porcelain doll. And then she smiled, breaking the illusion.

"I'm Alice." She held a hand out to me. "Welcome to your new home."

"You live in the barn?"

"No, silly," she said. "But I spend a lot of time here with my collection."

I peered around the barn from my position high on Bae's back. As my eyes adjusted to the dim light, I realized we weren't alone. An odd assortment of animals shuffled in the stalls.

"Come down, Gerda," she demanded. "I want to hear your story."

I slipped off the reindeer's back, but my legs buckled beneath me and I tumbled to the straw.

Before I could attempt to get to my feet, Alice settled on my lap, facing me. She wrapped her leather-clad legs around my waist and reached up to caress my face. "You are so beautiful," she said. "You remind me of the shadows dancing on the forest floor."

She tugged on my hair, drawing me down to her lips. I wanted to protest, to tell her about my quest, but I couldn't help myself. I wanted her more in that moment than I wanted to speak. I wasn't ready to share my defeat, my aimless quest to find Kay. I pushed the thoughts aside and dipped my head to breathe in the robber girl's scent. Alice parted her lips, but this time she let me take the lead. My tongue traced the curves of her face and then moved to explore the heat of her mouth. She sucked on my tongue and I groaned, pulling her close.

She pushed me on my back and straddled my hips, looking down at me with eyes the color of a twilight sky. "Where did you come from?"

"South," I replied, frustrated.

"I can see that." She delicately traced the curve of my jaw. "How far south? I've never seen anyone with skin the color of yours."

The scent of hay competed with the tang of winter in the barn. Something rustled high above in the rafters. I closed my eyes and thought of home: the deep forests, cultivated fields, and lofty castles. Then I reached farther back to my earliest memories of colored silks, perfumed gardens, and southern seas.

"Gerda?"

"I had a different name once."

Alice shifted her weight off my hips and slithered into the hay beside me. "What was it?"

"I don't remember."

Her hand slipped into mine. "Tell me."

I opened my eyes and peered into the cavernous dark overhead. The small windows in the barn doors were crusted with frost, distorting the little bit of light leaking into the large room.

"My first memories were of my grandmother. She lived in a

little cottage near the woods. We only had a few neighbors with children my age. There was Neva, the first girl I ever loved, and there was Kay." I sighed and pulled my fingers from hers.

"Is Neva who you are traveling to see?" Her question was tinged with dark regret.

I rolled on my side and looked her in the eye. "Neva is dead. My grandmother caught us together. She said our relationship was forbidden."

"What happened?"

"The next day, Neva disappeared." I sighed and reached out to touch the robber girl's cheek. "I was told the wolves got her."

Alice reached up to clasp my hand. "I'm sorry."

"I learned my lesson. I've never touched another woman again, until now."

The robber girl kissed me long and deep, tugging at my lips with her teeth until I opened my mouth for her to plunder.

After a moment, I gently pushed her away. "That's not the end of the story," I said, pressing my finger against her protest. "I may have put you in danger."

She grabbed my hand and pressed it against her breast. I shuddered at the touch of her firm breast in my palm. I curled my hand around the proud flesh and rubbed my thumb against the outline of the puckered bud.

"I am not afraid," she said.

"You should be." I lowered my hand and sat up in the straw. "My grandmother is the one who drove her away. I know it. She has the blood of wolves running through her veins." I paused and clenched my fists in my lap. "My grandmother forced me to marry Kay the next week. She didn't even let me have time to mourn the girl I loved."

"Is that why you're here? You ran away?"

"Not quite. I did as I was told. My grandmother told him of my love affair and warned him to keep me locked up so I couldn't attend to my 'unnatural' impulses." I shuddered. "He was no prince."

"I'm a prince," Bae said, tossing his antlers, proving his prowess.

"Shut up," said the robber girl.

I frowned. "Is he?"

"Yes," Bae said. "Kiss me and I will prove it."

"Go away before I decide to cut out your tongue."

Bae backed away, antlers bobbing back and forth as his disappeared into the gloom.

The robber girl snorted in disgust and looked back at me. "Don't listen to him. They all say the same thing."

"This is something I know. I learned it the hard way."

Alice reached out and began to caress my thigh. "How did you escape?"

I closed my eyes and concentrated on her soothing touch. "Neva."

Her hand pulled away. When I opened my eyes, the robber girl was standing over me with a murderous look on her face.

"Neva saved me." I smiled. "I saw her through the attic window. She pulled up in a sleigh pulled by thirty white geese. I could barely see her through the blizzard, but I know it was her. She called to him and Kay walked out of the house and into her arms."

"I thought you said she was dead." The robber girl began to pace.

"Maybe she was. Maybe it was her ghost who came to save me." I leaned back on my elbows and watched Alice circling me in those black thigh-high boots. "She once told me she originally lived in the Far North."

The robber girl stopped pacing and squatted down in front of me. "That's what you were doing in the thieves' woods? Heading north to find an old sweetheart?"

I stretched out and hooked my ankles around her calves, letting my skirts slide up to expose my legs. "No. I'm heading north to find Kay in the Snow Queen's castle." I leaned back into the hay and reached to tug my skirts even higher, revealing Kay's brand burned deep in my inner thigh. "I'm going to kill him for what he did to me."

The robber girl's eyes smoldered as her gaze raked over my exposed skin. She knelt between my legs and pushed my thighs apart. My breath caught in my throat and I closed my eyes, wondering if I'd made a mistake in trusting this strange woman I'd just met. There was no denying the spark between us, though. Neva and I had been budding girls when we began experimenting with pleasure. Despite Alice's small stature, she had a cunning strength about her that complemented the secret wolf bound at my core. If anyone could free me from my grandmother's curse, she was the one who could do it.

A rain of kisses scattered along the tender skin of my unmarked leg. Alice worked her way up, pushing the fabric of my skirt up around my hips as she went. I clenched my hands in the straw and held my breath as she approached my center. Light kisses brushed against my panties and then she began kissing her way down my other leg. When she got to the mark burned into the skin, she stopped. "He is a dead man," she said in a harsh whisper.

The cold steel of a knife's blade traced the lines spelling Kay's name. My eyes flew open and I shrank back. Alice's eyes had deepened to blue on the edge of black. Her pink lips stretched into a grimace exposing her unusually sharp teeth. I sensed a beast lurking within this small golden creature and wondered if I had made a mistake. Perhaps my grandmother had been right. Maybe my lust was an unnatural curse.

She lifted her head and scented the air. When she looked back at me, her face shifted. "I would never hurt you, Gerda."

She lifted the knife and tossed it aside. "But the man who did this to you will pay a terrible price."

Alice stood up and reached out a hand to help me to my feet. "Let's go inside the house. It's getting dark."

The animals, stabled in the shadowy recesses of the barn, shuffled in their stalls. Chains clinked among the whimpers and snorts. The sound of flapping wings and low moans made me eager to escape. I pushed my skirts down and took her hand. A shock of recognition passed between us and with it the realization that she'd known we were kindred spirits all along.

She laughed at my surprise. "Come along. You look hungry."

The blood of the wolf stirred in my veins. I wasn't hungry. I was starving.

Alice pulled me along behind her, giving me a perfect view of her round ass flexing under the cover of her tight black pants. I ran my tongue over my lips and sliced my tongue on a sharp canine. I frowned at the metallic taste of my own blood.

She pushed the barn door open and we raced across the snowy expanse to the cozy cottage. Lights burned in the windows. Overhead, the sun was racing toward the horizon in a blazing ball of burnt orange. A full moon had already started its ascent into the darkening sky. The pungent scent of pine trees tickled my nose. I didn't remember the smell being so strong earlier in the day. The wind shifted, blowing Alice's musky scent back to me. I breathed deep and smiled.

Inside the cottage, a fire burned in the hearth. Alice stalked through the lightly furnished front room, lighting candles as she went. Instead of furniture, colorful pillows were strewn across fur rugs, layered on the hardwood floor. The log walls were bare of decorations. In the adjoining kitchen, dried herbs and flowers hung from the ceiling, giving off an aromatic fragrance that complemented the smoking firewood.

"Take your shoes off and relax," said Alice. "I will be right back."

She disappeared into one of the cabin's back rooms. I kicked off my wet slippers and unclasped my cloak, letting it fall to the floor. The fireplace beckoned, so I walked across a white fur rug, enjoying the tickle of it underfoot, before dropping down into a makeshift bed of fluffy cushions. The fire was so hot as to be almost uncomfortable and it made me aware of the damp clamminess of my clothing. I glanced across the room, but Alice still hadn't returned, so I tugged off my blouse, and shimmied out of my outer skirt and tossed them to the side. I tugged a fur over the thin linen of my slip and settled back into the pillows. I closed my eyes and sighed.

I woke to a gentle kiss pressed on my cheek. My eyes flared open to find Alice pressed up against me.

"You were sleeping when I came out of the bathroom, so I made something to snack on," she said, gesturing to a low table filled with small plates of sliced cheese, smoked fish, seeded crackers, and dried fruit.

I stretched and realized I could use a bathroom myself. "Would you mind if I clean up a bit first?"

"Go ahead." She smiled. "I drew a bath for you. I hope you like lavender."

I sniffed her neck. "If that's what you used, I'll love it."

"It's the second door to the right. I will build up the fire while you're gone."

I shrugged off the fur and watched to see her reaction to my general state of undress, but she had already turned away and was sitting on her knees preparing to tend the fire. Frustrated, I walked to the bathroom and opened the door. A lovely copper tub steamed invitingly. Without shutting the door, I tugged off my remaining clothes and slipped into the water. It was heaven.

I spent my time working soap through my hair and rinsing

the straw and dirt from my dark curls. With a cloth she'd left draped over the edge of the tub, I soaped my body, spending extra time on my breasts and between my legs. I lingered on my clit, gently rubbing the nub with my forefinger, wishing Alice would come in to watch me bathe, but she never walked through the door and the water began to cool. Instead of finding relief, my touch only increased my need. I dried off with a towel and looked at my clothes, crumpled in a heap on the floor. The thought of putting them back on was unbearable. I wanted to feel fur covering my bare skin. With a boldness I'd thought lost years ago, I walked out of the bathroom naked except for the towel slung around my hips.

Alice looked at me then. She lounged in the cushions and was nibbling on dried apricots when I entered the room. I stopped, standing on a black fur, as her eyes devoured me. She set the plate aside and rose to her feet. Her tits strained against a tightly laced red shirt. A short, matching skirt revealed strong legs, which flexed as she stalked me from across the room in those sexy black boots.

I froze in place, thrilled with the feeling of being naked in front of her. Dampness began to seep between my legs when she stopped in front of me.

"Drop the towel."

I complied. My nipples puckered like black cherries. She bent down and flicked her tongue across the ripe buds cresting my heavy breasts. I moaned and reached up to cradle her head. Alice pulled away and laughed wickedly.

"Tell me what you want."

I shook my head and thrust my breasts toward her. *Suck me, please.* But I couldn't say the words. I hadn't been allowed to express my desires for years and I was afraid the darkness inside of me would frighten this blonde creature away.

Her sapphire eyes darkened. "Get down on your knees."

I shuddered, but crouched down on all fours and stared at the black fur beneath me. I could smell her excitement seeping between her legs. My canines lengthened in my mouth. Alice knelt behind me and pressed up against the flesh of my bare ass. She reached around and began to massage my breasts, clever fingers milking my tits. With each stroke, she would flick the nipples with her thumbs until they ached with longing. I wanted her hot lush mouth pressed against my breasts, her sharp little teeth teasing the tender buds. *Please.*

She stopped. I almost howled in disappointment. My head lifted in protest, but she pushed my chest into the floor with one strong hand and reached between my thighs with the other. Her fingers parted the dusky curls and stroked the heat hidden in my center. She stroked deep inside, followed by the slick curve of a finger reaching up to press against my clit. At the end of each caress, Alice flicked the sensitive tip, pinching it gently, before sliding back to stroke me again. The pleasure swelled and I pushed back into her hand, attempting to increase the pace. *Harder. Faster. Please.*

Abruptly, Alice let go of me and moved away.

"No," I howled and turned to pounce on her, hold her down, ravage her. Alice watched me with a cool grace, her legs spread wide to reveal her golden down and the hint of pink promising to quench my hunger.

With a speed that shocked me, I rushed forward and bent my head to smell her sex. Her desire glistened on the golden curls and I dipped my head to taste her. She tasted like a honey-drenched peach, and I sucked and licked every inch, seeking every drop of that golden nectar. Alice moaned and thrust against me, taking more of my tongue into her tight core. I pressed a finger into her ass, stroking every inch of her. When my teeth scraped against her clit, Alice arched her back and cried out with the orgasm ripping through her.

I sat up and ripped her skirt away with sharp claws.

Alice panted past a grin. "Tell me what you want."

I growled and tore at her bodice, eager to shred the red silk to expose her breasts. She reached down. Her fingernails shifted into clawed talons, which she used to cut through the laces. I leaned forward, my heavy breasts pressing against her stomach. I ached for release, but I stopped to suckle the little pink rosebuds cresting her small tits.

She reached down to fondle my nipples in turn and I groaned. "Alice."

With an unnatural strength, she pushed me off of her and rolled to straddle my hips. Her leather boots rubbed against my thighs. "Tell me."

"Suck on me," I begged. "Please."

Alice grinned, exposing her sharp little teeth as she dipped her head to do my bidding. She sucked and pinched and tugged on my nipples, her hands milking my heavy flesh. I groaned and writhed underneath her as an orgasm built in my center. "Oh yes, please," I shouted, arching my back. She bit down. The intense pleasure peaked. I howled, hands clasped tight in the fur bunched under my back.

I panted, attempting to catch my breath, but she decided to breathe for me, kissing me with the deep stroking of her tongue. She grasped my hair in her fists and plundered my mouth as she ground her pussy against mine. I bucked to meet her insistence and grabbed her waist to pull her closer, but Alice had other ideas. She slithered out of my grasp and twisted around, pushed my thighs apart, and nuzzled my sex, dipping her tongue past my curls to tease my clit.

I groaned and dug my fingers into the firm flesh of her ass. She pushed down harder, sucking my swollen flesh with teasing tugs. I spread the cheeks of her ass and dipped my fingers into her pink wetness, matching her rhythm. Relentless, she sucked and probed every crest and valley between my legs before she settled back to tongue my clit as I fucked her pussy with my hand. The pressure built until I felt as though I couldn't bear the pleasure another minute. Alice bucked against me, her tightness clamping down on the thrusting fingers. At the same time, she lightly nipped my clit and then tugged on it with her lips. Pleasure ripped through me. Alice's orgasm dripped down my arm to pool on my breasts. She sighed and collapsed on top of me.

For a few moments, we lay tangled together, spent. The fire crackled, its fuel nearly gone. The room was dim and filled with the musky scent of sex. Alice rolled to her back and then curled at my side. I tugged a fur over our legs and stroked her back. A purr rumbled deep in her chest.

"Tell me you'll stay," Alice murmured.

"I'll stay."

She stretched out at my side, molding her body against my curves. "Tell me you won't leave me behind when you go after Kay."

The wolf inside me grinned. "Who's Kay?"

# THE PRINCESS'S PRINCESS

## Salome Wilde

I do not often find opportunity to indulge in remembrance of my youth. I have lived long and held great power. I have been generous and mean, wise and foolhardy. Yet, I have loved only once. The pleasures of my first romance are the stuff of dreams, and they deserve a place among my memoirs. Alongside war diaries and the signing of monumental decrees, there must also be Jiin. When all else fades from my memory, there will be Jiin.

Two days after the birthday that rendered me a full adult in the eyes of the kingdom, I was sitting in my ridiculously well-appointed chambers, avoiding my studies after having dismissed my tutor and lamenting the burdens my parents the king and queen placed upon me as heir to the throne. The Lord High Chamberlain interrupted my thoughts, announcing himself and requesting entrance. He said he had brought someone to meet me at the behest of my father. I bade him enter, welcoming the diversion. He produced a lovely young woman whose looks made it plain she was from a distant land. Her skin was rich

with bronze shadows. Her gaze was soft. As he guided her into
the room, I casually concluded she was to be my new servant.
Surely she was a tribute to my family from some kingdom that
needed our good will or our troops or some other favor that did
not and need not concern me. I had experienced little else of
nations other than my own.

The girl was clad in lush silks and sparkling baubles. Golden
bracelets ran from wrist nearly to elbow on each arm; tiny
gilded mirrors glinted from a broad, midnight-blue silk sash
over her shoulder. Her lowered eyelids glittered, and her ankles
were painted with elaborate shining swirls. She even had a tiny
gold crown atop her black, ornately wrapped hair. But I did not
see a magnificent, royal-born creature before me: all I saw was
a beautifully wrapped gift. I commanded the girl to sit on the
rug at the foot of my bed, and she did so, while the Chamberlain
gasped and gawped.

"Your Majesty..." he stammered.

Both Jiin and I replied, "Yes?" at the same instant, Jiin with
the lilt of a sensuous foreign tongue. I looked down at her and
she up at me. I can only imagine now the glare of immature fury
that appeared on my face at that moment. Was the girl mocking
me?

He began again, "Forgive me, *Majesties*—I meant Princess
Jiin."

"Princess?" I burst out, glaring at the Chamberlain. Why
had he not told me the moment she entered? He had humiliated
me! But no, I rashly decided, it was not he who had wronged
me but *she*!

I slowly returned my gaze to this "Princess" Jiin, who
continued to look up at me from her lowly position on the floor.
Her feet were neatly tucked beneath her, hands in her lap, like
the most obedient and well trained of serving girls. I knew *I*
would never sit so. Why had she done it? To make me feel the

fool: there was no other explanation. "You are a princess?" I asked in a quietly threatening voice.

"One is," she replied with a nod, humble and soft-spoken as I myself never was.

"Well, get up then! A princess should never abase herself so." I thought that if I acted outraged enough, perhaps the Chamberlain would not tell everyone in the castle that I had made an ass of myself before visiting royalty.

Jiin rose silently and nimbly. I envied every inch of her graceful, modest demeanor. And I hated her for it, and for the indirect way she referred to herself as "One."

"One has a gift for Your Highness," she offered, adding insult to injury, removing a gold ring from a tiny pouch she wore at her waist.

The item was ornately wrought, seeming to suggest the figure of a woman, twisted around in a perfect circle, hands reaching up between her legs. It seemed an odd gift to me, when surely the Princess's land had *some* precious gem they might instead have fashioned atop the little band. They must be a poor country, I rashly concluded. I tried not to show my disappointment, knowing the Chamberlain was watching and that I already looked an idiot. ("Never wear your emotions in your eyes," my father always told me. "Wear your power with ease not struggle.")

"I thank you, Princess—." I stopped short, for I did not remember her name. Again, I was at a disadvantage, and, again, I did not like it a bit.

"This is Princess Jiin of Dinzhan," the Chamberlain chimed in. "His Majesty the King has invited Princess Jiin and her mother, Queen Yiin, to stay in the palace for a time. A great treaty between our kingdom and theirs will mean greater prosperity for..."

I tuned out the words of the paunchy, pompous fool, focused

as I was on regaining the upper hand in this situation. "I thank
you, Princess *Jiin*," I began again, clipping the end of the Chamberlain's sentence, "for your generous gift. We are honored to
have you within our humble walls." That should fix her. Our
castle was glorious, huge, and ornate, the grandest in our land
or any other, I surmised with infinite arrogance and utter ignorance. She merely smiled and bowed.

After that first meeting, my coldness toward the sneaky, too-
humble Jiin kept us far apart except when necessary. I main-
tained what I thought of as an air of dignity and aloofness
but no doubt appeared as petulance. She, by contrast, seemed
always to have an indulgent smile on her face that made me feel
immature and foolish. I disliked her immensely.

A few weeks into their stay, Queen Yiin formally presented
my father with a vast, elaborate wall-hanging that depicted a
map of her kingdom—which turned out to be thrice the size
of my father's. I fumed but had to attend the ceremony. As I
gaped at the tapestry, I felt my earlier condescension with an
inward cringe that I could only hope would not show outwardly
as the radiant Jiin smiled into my eyes and said, as if we were
continuing a conversation from our first meeting, "And these
are *this one's* humble walls."

I muttered, "Humble indeed," in response to her taunt in the
guise of false modesty, and she murmured back, "That is just
what this one was going to say."

"Twit," I snapped.

"Brat," she hissed.

"Idiot."

"Child."

With that, we suddenly found we had everyone's attention in
the room. My father's stern glare was mirrored in the eyes of my
mother and Jiin's. We were in trouble. But Jiin spoke up immediately: "Please forgive these childish games, Your Highnesses.

The Princess and this one are just like sisters; and thus, like sisters, we squabble. The outburst was this one's fault entirely." And she made a pretty little bow that had my father and the two queens beaming.

My competitive streak had me wanting to outdo the princess in humility, of course, but I could not think of anything to say. I was too proud to fake it. So, I reached out and embraced her. At first she stood, stiff as a pike: not only had we never hugged, we had never so much as touched. But then she softened, wrapped her arms around me, and brought her lips to my cheek for a kiss. I felt a tingle and marveled at it. Before I could make more of the strange sensation, however, Jiin had moved her mouth to my ear and whispered, "You are no child to have such soft, lush *lukshas*."

I was entirely shocked as she released me, but there was no question that *lukshas* meant my bosom, which she had pressed against so warmly. The tingle quickly became a flush down my throat and out to the tips of my heretofore-unnoticed breasts. They were only of average size and I had never thought them special, but to Jiin they were apparently worthy of comment. I relished the praise more than I could say and for a reason I could not name. In fact, I cannot remember anything else that was said as we hung the tapestry in the Great Hall that day, and I retreated to my chambers as swiftly as I could when dismissed. I think my mother quipped something about my looking chilled, but I could not remember ever feeling more overheated.

Back in my rooms, I began to rethink the matter in my barely adult way. What did Jiin mean by her remarks? Was she simply taunting me, increasing the stakes in our ridiculous rivalry? That did not ring true, and I did not want it to be true. That Jiin's voice had been a soft, lusty purr unlike any voice ever addressed to me only made me more confused. I decided the only way to resolve my feeling of discomfort was to confront her. I made my way down the long hallway to Jiin's rooms, passing a chamber-maid and a guard, both of whom I was sure could see the stirred fluster in my bearing, though neither did more than show the usual signs of deference to their princess.

When I burst into Jiin's room without so much as a pause to knock, she turned from her work with a gasp. She was painting a nude female, and her model, sitting on a small platform oppo-site her, seemed to be one of the palace chamber servants. The creature's red-gold cloud of hair was done up with the kind of decoration Jiin wore, and her plump pale arms sported brace-lets like Jiin's. The servant quickly reached for a cloth to cover herself. Worse, I could tell there had been some light merriment in conversation that I had interrupted. The woman lowered her eyes, and asked Jiin quietly if she should go.

"Forgive me for intruding, Princess," I said, too loudly, feeling foolish and out of place. I turned to leave.

"Please, do not go," Jiin hastily replied. "It is time that one gives a break to one's companion from the dull work of modeling. Thank you, Dani." She smiled warmly and the servant smiled back through lowered lashes and bowed.

I saw the friendship between them and was hotly envious. I would never have spoken with such affection to a servant, or even to others, like the Chamberlain, to whom I owed respect. And that Jiin even knew the creature's name was mortifying. My father had taught me haughtiness—perhaps more than he meant to—and it had left me alone and standoffish. Yet, here was Princess Jiin, my equal in stature and my superior in matu-rity, gentility, beauty, and tact, and I had thrown away a chance at friendship with her. I flushed again and, again, felt my nipples tighten beneath my garments.

The servant slipped out the door at the back of the room, bowing as she went. I stood, waiting for Jiin to speak again. As she fiddled with her paints, I took in the room around me, a room that I had perhaps ventured into a time or two in my life but to which I had paid little attention, save to note its similarity to so many guest chambers in the palace. Jiin had transformed it. With sheer draperies, a musky incense that lent a smoky warmth to the room, and tapestries like the one her mother had given to my parents but featuring unfamiliar landscapes and unfamiliar birds of bright plumage, Jiin had made this cold, high-ceilinged chamber her own. I turned back to note more closely her work area in the corner, full of paints, brushes, and canvases.

"Would you like to model?" Jiin asked, bringing me out of my reverie, her voice low and playful.

"M-me?" I stammered, shocked but uncharacteristically tempted, lured by the delicious note of seduction in Jiin's sweetly accented voice. "You want me to...let you paint me?" I could not say the final phrase—"without my clothes"—nor could I imagine she meant this. Though the servant Jiin had taken as her model was of low station, she was surprisingly lovely. Even as the idea that status did not determine beauty or grace flashed through my mind for the very first time, I felt Jiin's eyes upon me and rankled at the restrictiveness of my heavy, royal garments.

Jiin came to me and took my hand, laughing lightly. Her face was radiant with mirth; her eyes sparkled and her fingertips were delicate and warm. Her dark skin, a shade deeper than mine, was lustrous. How could I not have noticed the princess's exquisite fineness? How could I have thought myself higher than this goddess?

I let her guide me to the tiny dais the servant model had been sitting on. It was draped with rich sable furs. How delicious it would feel on my bare backside, I thought, shocked at myself.

"Do not blush, sister," Jiin whispered. "Though it looks well on you."

I brought my fingers to my reddening cheeks to hide them

from Jiin's acute gaze. I felt a child again; it seemed I could not stop feeling immature and foolish in front of this infernal woman.

"Would you truly display yourself for one's brush?" Jiin teased, bringing the tip of a paintbrush to play across her finger-tips. "As you can see, one's talents are meager, but the art is only as good as the subject, *kaa*?" She winked, and gently brushed the tip of my nose.

I smiled, despite myself, and gazed up at her. I was a silly little fly, caught in the elegant web of her silken words and sensuous movements. I began unlacing the front of my gown, my eyes never leaving Jiin's. My effort was absurdly clumsy, for I was accustomed to being dressed by others, and my mind suddenly flew to the difference between showing bare flesh to a serving girl and to Jiin.

She watched me closely, and her expression said that she was as shocked at my undressing as I was to be doing it. But she did not stop me. Instead, she gently assisted me, smiling softly where I frowned, loosening laces I had knotted. When at last I slipped my shoulders from the sleeves and stood before her, bare-breasted, I felt the thrill of sexual self-awareness as I never had before. I turned slightly and dared to look at myself in the mirror. The sun poured in through the open casement opposite, and the light was uncompromising. Yet, imagining Jiin's gaze, I rejected the usual imperfections I hunted for in my adolescent reflection. Instead, I saw an auburn-haired girl with rich, bronzed skin, wide, narrow eyes, softly parted lips, and maturing breasts with large dusky nipples that ached for a touch. Could I reach my hands up and feel them myself? Better still: could I somehow get Jiin to embrace me again?

But I was not so brave as to make it so. I turned my eyes back to Jiin, who was now sucking on the end of her paintbrush, eyes fastened on my navel. Her eyes flickered, then met mine.

There was such heat there it made me blush harder—if that was possible. She returned again to looking at my belly then back up to my eyes. And soon I realized that her gaze was settling lower: she wanted to see all of me. I swallowed hard and bit my lip. Her smile widened. She was obviously seeing my apprehension and enjoying that, too. A trace of childish competitiveness surfaced again and decided my actions. I roughly widened the lacing at my waist, then pushed the fabric down over my slender hips, letting it drop heavily down my legs and to the floor.

Then I was paralyzed. I had been naked in front of serving girls for as long as I could remember. They not only dressed me but washed and dried me, powdered and adorned me, brushed and styled my hair. But they never stood, hand on hip, devouring me with their eyes. They would not dare—nor perhaps desire to. But Jiin dared, as she had with that servant. And thinking about that servant model did a surprising thing for me at that moment: it freed me. I imagined I was simply Jiin's model, a young woman with no pretensions to power or prestige. The princess could do anything she wanted with me and I would let her. I would glory in the honor of offering myself to her. I unbound my hair and shook it free, a cascade of unruly curls. I bit my lip as I let my eyelids softly close to await Jiin's touch.

When it came, after a slight rustling of her skirts that made my flesh prickle and my breath quicken, I was more completely unprepared than I had thought it possible to be. Her hands cupped both of my breasts, weighing them gently; then she left only her thumbs there and began to move them in tiny circles. My nipples tingled and the tingle rapidly became an ache. Jiin seemed to know the effects she was causing, and began to gently roll my left nipple with finger and thumb. As that gesture became a rhythmic pressing, I suddenly felt her hand on my sex. She had nimbly slipped fingers down and gently opened me in a way I had never imagined. I gasped and jumped back, tripping over my bunched-up gown and falling on my backside.

Jiin made her own little gasp, and came to help me up. "Oh! Are you all right?"

I was so embarrassed that, as I scrambled to get back to my feet, all I managed to do was become more entangled in my clothing. Without grace or patience, I finally kicked free of the garment and ran for the door. Heaven only knew where my brains had gone to, but thankfully Jiin still had hers. "Stop!" she shouted as I put my hand on the handle to let myself out.

I turned and looked at Jiin, her face a mask of anxious concern. Only when reflected in her eyes did I realize that I was about to head out into the hall, completely undressed. The scandal would have been terrible, perhaps ruinous to Jiin's stay, and mortifying to my parents, not to mention me. I rushed back to my gown and hastily tried to dress, wishing Jiin would stop watching me. She came over quietly and put her hand on my bare shoulder. I felt the rush of arousal again and tried to move out of her reach without being obvious.

"Princess," she said, grasping me more firmly by both shoulders and turning me to face her. She kissed me then, sweetly and firmly, and it both stirred and calmed me. Then she spoke again. "One is so sorry if one frightened you—"

"No—" I began, wanting to stop Jiin from saying something that would embarrass me further.

But she shook her head and continued, her voice rich as honey. "Let us not push ourselves too quickly. Let us seek pleasures we can give ourselves...together, *kaa*?"

I did not know what she meant, but I knew I would not flee again. She took my hand and guided me to her bed, draped with silks of the same midnight blue she always wore. Could any color have set off the bronzed glow of her skin better? I could not imagine it, especially as she stood on the bed before me—so high was the canopy that she could do so—upon the tousled linen. Had her model trespassed here, too? I doubted that, but would not think further on it. Unwrapping the winding cloth from her torso, she revealed her perfect small breasts and slender, muscled arms. Her shoulders were broad, as were her hips. She was magnificent, a dark, golden goddess I longed for but feared to worship with my whole body and soul. As I leaned back on a plump feather pillow, I feigned an ease in watching her disrobe that I desperately wished I could feel. But Jiin did not betray her awareness of my nervousness if she sensed it. Instead, she stood on the bed, and in that gauze-draped space of shadowed warmth, she revealed herself to me in a seductive, undulating dance.

Her fingers kissed her flesh as her arms waved, like the most graceful of serpents. With wrists that bent and turned elegantly, she beckoned with her paint-spattered hands, first downturned then palms-up, inviting me to watch her every movement. Below, her hips swayed softly and rhythmically, freeing her waist until her ample skirts slid down to her ankles. Each new inch of flesh enflamed me, and I grew from anxious to eager to passionate, until finally she stood before me, a glittering creature of fantasy, lithe and wide-hipped, a mysterious being of unearthly beauty.

When she at last let her legs fold gracefully beneath her to sit beside me, I could scarcely breathe. Her breath, too, came fast, I noted, and I could feel its warmth on my cheek as she leaned nearer. Her body arched toward me. She placed a kiss on my cheek as her hand reached between my legs. I stiffened without meaning to. She withdrew and sat back, as if this was exactly what she had planned.

I reddened anew, ashamed that I was so shy with someone I so wished to please. I felt I had rejected her dreadfully, but she did not show signs of being either upset or disappointed. I

opened my mouth to speak, but she put two fingers to my lips
and I forbore. I did find the strength to press a kiss to her tender
digits, and this made her smile. She then pushed back a bit and
made herself comfortable, legs bent at the knee, facing me. She
leaned on some pillows behind her, propping herself up on one
slender elbow and spreading her smooth thighs. I watched; I
could not look away. She nodded her head, bidding me silently
to pose as she was. I obeyed.

She placed two fingers in her mouth and sucked softly on
them, holding my eyes. I was puzzled yet aroused at the sight.
She nodded again, and I came to understand that I was to do
everything she did. I slipped two fingers into my mouth, feeling
less foolish than I had anticipated, so mesmerized was I. And
when she then took her wet digits from between her lips and
reached them down between her legs, I knew I must do this, too.
I felt dizzy and unsure, but I obeyed.

She spoke then, her voice breaking into the silence but in a
tone as hypnotizing as her movements: "Before you can enjoy
the touch of others, lovely princess, you must enjoy your own.
Gardens of pleasure are our bodies. Ripe, fleshy fruit are our
mouths. Both fruit and tight bud are our breasts; a full bloom
is our sex. Part the petals, sweet one, and explore the dewy
warmth of your blossoming flower." Her eyes drifted shut as she
coaxed herself apart with first finger and pinky, then brought
her two middle fingers to open her glistening inner lips. I saw
between them a tiny bud, which she massaged in little circles,
alternating with occasional dips into her core, where her fingers
were wetted, producing soft sighs that I echoed. She spread her
legs more widely and stretched them, and I tingled where her
thighs brushed against mine.

As her sighs became exquisite moans, I began to stroke
myself gently. I did not look down, afraid to miss a moment of
Jiin's beautiful self-pleasuring and still awkward with my own

body. I gasped as I watched her bloom and swell, the flesh of her sex reddening to a ripe, burgundy blush.

I found the parts of my sex that I had never gazed upon, never toyed with. I wondered for a brief moment why I had not, what had kept me from loving myself as Jiin did herself. Why had I not come to know my own body? I felt curling pubic hair, plump outer labia, moist inner folds, and my own hidden nub. I jumped as I rubbed it: a shy bud that needed the lightest of touches. And as I explored, I never took my eyes from Jiin's fingers.

Suddenly, she gasped, her muscles locking as her teeth sank into her bottom lip. I did not stop touching myself as she stroked furiously, on a path of pleasure I desperately wanted to follow. "Jiin," I whispered, as she lay back more fully and brought her other hand to pump fingers in and out of her opening. She cried out in pleasure. Her body began to shake, then arched hard and I sensed a sudden bursting within her. I marveled at her movements and sounds—a new dance, the like of which I had never before seen—and envied what she must be feeling.

Her trembling lessened and her fingers stopped thrusting, and she sighed and shivered all over. I came to her side and wrapped myself around her. I wanted somehow to comfort her though I knew she was not in distress. I clung to her body, damp with beads of sweat, kissing her ear, neck, and shoulder. I tasted her salt and her sweetness. She accepted my tribute, giggling softly as her body rocked with tiny spasms. Then she threw her arms around me and pressed the whole of our bodies together. "Precious innocent," she murmured. "Did you enjoy one's display?"

I nodded, sheepishly, into her neck, feeling far younger than my years.

Jiin stretched her lithe frame and bade me sit up. "Will you offer the same for this one?" she purred.

I rose but shook my head. "I...do not think I..."

"Of course you can," she interrupted, putting rich-smelling fingers to my lips. I kissed them. She laughed again, and I knew it for pleasure. How could I ever have thought she had mocked me? "One shall tell you a secret."

I nodded, our gazes locked. *Oh, tell me a secret,* I pleaded with my eyes. *Tell me all your secrets, incomparable goddess!*

"You can please yourself better than anyone else. Enjoy the touch of others when you are ready, but now give this gift to yourself." She took my hand in hers and brought it between my legs. "Just touch yourself, my Princess, and see what pleases you." She removed her hand but kept her eyes on mine. "Go on, lovely one: soon you will find your way."

I closed my eyes and pressed my hand to cup my sex, felt the prickling of the small tuft of hair. I worried I would not be able to do as she had done, not reach the ecstasy she seemed to find so easily. I worried she would grow displeased or, worse, disinterested. But I took a deep breath and sighed it out, determined to meet this challenge for my goddess. If I was very lucky, I would feel some small bit of the pleasure she had experienced for herself and offer it up to her. I squeezed myself gingerly, and felt the heat there.

"One will so enjoy watching you," she whispered, encouraging me as if she had read my thoughts. And though her words should have brought me more embarrassment, they did not now. I felt moisture pool and brought my fingers to my slickened entrance. I pressed my two middle fingers inside, as Jiin had done, and I was rewarded with a shudder of arousal. I was soft and wet inside—a juicy, pulpy fruit—warm and welcoming. I had never entered myself this way, and again I marveled at that fact. Whose body was this but my own? Who else should plumb its depths, riper than I had ever imagined? I withdrew my fingers until only the tips were left inside, then drove them in more forcefully and felt a rush of heat and wetness. It made me giggle. This was good. I smiled to myself, eyes closed tightly, and was urged on by the sound of Jiin's soft moan. I longed to look upon her face, but I feared I would break the spell of my own wantonness if I raised my eyelids.

I continued to delve, fingers thrusting in and out; then brought my right hand to join my left, spreading my lips and tracing circles around and across that tiny node of pleasure, which I quickly found again. I grew dizzy from the rush of sensation and from the exertion of making my hands do as my excitement demanded. I labored long, growing frustrated when the building arousal waned and shocked with delight when it again grew and kept growing. Soon, I lost track of anything but the needs of my body, centered in the fiery core of me. I arched into my own hands as though it was not I who brought this pleasure but Jiin, my muscles tightening and my legs spreading wide of their own accord. My flesh ripened and swelled around my eager fingers, fingers far nimbler than I ever knew them to be. And after what felt an eternity of rising and falling and rising again, I felt a sharpening of my senses, a drawing in of all my energies. All of my blood was flowing to my sex. All of the universe was entering into me, until my entire being was a knot of unendurable tightness. My body opened like a flower thirsting for a downpour. My fingers were numb and I ached for release, for something I could not name but which approached with increasing force from just beyond my reach.

Suddenly it hit. I peaked with the explosion of thunder in the heavens. I was torn as lightning splits a tree. I was... But, oh, I cannot do it justice. Such words pale by comparison to the experience, as all who have experienced the body's bliss know only too well. When I reopened my eyes, Jiin's smile was so broad and ripe that I knew we had shared this pleasure as fully as if we had touched each other instead of ourselves. She had given my body and my desire to me even as she partook of every moment through her rapt attention. I would be forever grateful.

Gratitude, however, was not my primary emotion as she embraced and celebrated my blossoming with me. We kissed and fondled as I trembled all over. We laughed and scrambled under plush blankets to warm our exposed flesh. And we would have kept this up for hours had Jiin not noted the position of the sun in the sky—it was nearly sunset. I leapt from the bed and Jiin helped me dress with haste so I could return to my chambers and dress for the evening banquet. It would not do to disappoint our parents and give away our secret. We parted with a kiss and my promise to return when the moon was high. It was a promise we kept, as we kept a thousand promises during that visit.

Now, so many years later that I am loath to count them, I chronicle my life, and the Jiin of my budding adulthood returns to me. She comes to me in visions of royal blue, dark eyes shining and brown arms open to summon me. Though I have forgotten many a day and will no doubt forget more as time continues to pass, I can never forget Jiin. I may be an aging noble who was once a naïve young princess, but I am also all that passed between youth and old age. And I am privileged beyond measure for having met Jiin and felt her love.

"Life offers more pleasures than one can count, if one only allows," as Jiin, my consort of more than sixty years now, so often reminds me.

# WOODWITCH

## M. Birds

By their third day on the move, a number of women had started to follow the army, walking steadily behind the progressing ranks of men on horseback. Some carried squalling babes against their breasts or bound across their backs, some pulled wagons behind them. Some were old and stoop shouldered, some painted with kohl and rouge and dressed in lace.

"Camp followers," one of the soldiers told the princess, with a curl of his lip. "Looking to sell their bodies or scavenge the dead. More trouble than they're worth. Come the battle, they'll be wanting protection, and we've little enough of that to spare."

At night, the princess lay awake in her canvas tent and listened to the groans of pleasure from the tents around her, mingled with the usual snores and cries. Men were a loud bunch, at rest or no. They would meet the enemy tomorrow or the next day; blood would not be put off for long. She felt her sword hand clench around empty air. Only two weeks as a knight, and she ached without a blade to hold.

On their fourth day, a dark-haired woman joined the

followers' ranks, lingering just at the edges of the slow-moving crowd. She had a mass of tangled hair, a hooked nose, and thin, rose-red lips. Strange runes and symbols were inked across her arms and the palm of her left hand was painted green.

"A woodwitch," a soldier told the princess, before spitting on the ground. "They stain their hands to show they serve the earth. An ill omen, she is. They honor no kings, and have no loyalty."

The princess studied the witch as she walked beside her, the slant of her mouth, the crease of her thick eyebrows. The witch did not look back.

By the end of that day's march, rumor of the witch had spread through the ranks, and there was much talk at supper of killing her while she slept, or seeing how much gold it would take for her to spread her legs like a common woman. The princess had nothing to say to this. After a fortnight spent training and living alongside these men, she was used to such talk. She ate her dried meat and hard bread in silence, the mockery turning to thunder, only thunder, rolling in the distance.

By the fifth day, the woodwitch had an eye bruised green and purple, and the enemy was upon them.

Once upon a time, when magic ran like fault lines through the earth, a daughter was born to a great king. She was not the princess of songs and stories; flaxen haired, fine boned, fairest of them all. No, this princess was tall and strong, and her mother died giving life to her. She was raised by her brothers, more at ease on a horse than a throne, and could wield a sword more skillfully by ten than many men by twenty. She had a strong jaw and a sweet voice, and many said (with hushed tones and pitying eyes) that she was the very image of her father in his boyhood.

These were times of violence in the kingdom, for the princess's father had been at war with the king to the south for nearly twenty years. One by one, the princess's brothers waved to her as they rode off to battle, and one by one their bodies were sent back, wrapped in golden shrouds. Rarely did they die on horseback, for the enemy was craven and unnatural. The South favored sorcery to swords, and the princess's brothers died of fever, died coughing, died vomiting from sicknesses no godly man could name. Rumors spread that the king's line was cursed, that none of his seed would ever ride away from battle. The king grew bitter and vicious in his grief, locked himself in his chambers for months on end, and still men fought for him, and still men died.

The princess saw her father for the last time on her twenty-first birthday. He came to her bedchamber, found her hunch shouldered and sullen after fighting with her handmaids for the hundredth time. Her corsets were too loose about the chest, too tight about the hips. Her skirts were torn from riding; her fine dresses misshapen from the strength of her shoulders and her arms.

"It would have been better if you were a boy," the king said, voice leathery as the covers of long-forgotten books. "You might have been a soldier, then. Might have fought for me as your brothers did."

The princess turned from her mirror to see him standing in her doorway, beard tangled and gaze dull. She had loved her brothers, but there was a time when she had loved him most of all—loved to hear him speak of death and honor, loved the blue fire of his eyes as he toasted the downfall of their enemies, the red wine that spilled like blood from the corners of his mouth.

"It would be better had you been a boy," the king said, "than the creature you are."

"What creature is that?" the princess asked, voice shaking.

"I would rather have no heirs at all, than one daughter who does not know her place."

The door closed behind the king, but to the princess's ears it sounded like the falling of an axe.

She had watched her brothers ride away so many times, knew the prideful angle of their jaws and the stiff arch of their spines. She could lift a longsword with one hand, and still throw a dagger in the other. She took one of those daggers now, and raised it to her throat. It ran like water through her thick blonde hair, carving it off easily below her ears. When she tilted her jaw and arched her back, she barely recognized herself. She had no breasts to bind, but she bound them anyway. Then she stole her brother's leather and mail, found a swift horse and a dull sword, and went off to break a curse.

The battle raged for the rise and fall of two moons, and when at last the enemy ran staggering from their sight, the princess found herself slick with sweat and blood. She had cut down two men, she knew that much. Maybe more. One had his throat slit open, wet red roses blooming over the dry earth. One had her sword buried in his belly, opened up around her blade like rotten meat. The princess had been sick after that, but the ground was so mired in filth, the air so ripe with smoke, that no one had taken any notice of her.

There were fewer of her number than before, and as she stood amidst the thinned crowd of the injured and the dying, she realized that her leg was bleeding.

Cursing, she tore a strip from her tunic. The cut was high and deep, rending both skin and muscle. Even as she bound it, blood spilled from the bandage like dark fingers, the pain enough to make her dizzy. She had felt numb before, fueled only by pure and terrified survival, but in the aftermath of battle all her injuries were making themselves known. Her muscles screamed with exhaustion, her ribs throbbed where she had been kicked. She took a hesitant step, and felt bile at the back of her throat.

She wondered if her brothers had felt like this after battle. She wondered if she was a true knight now, now that she had stopped a man's heart.

"That wound needs seeing to."

The princess did not know who spoke until she noticed the dark-haired witch a few yards away, moving like a dancer between the crows and carrion. The princess ignored her, pulling the binding tighter. The witch was not looking at her, crouched and peering into the mouth of a fallen soldier. When she jerked her arm, the princess realized she was pulling teeth from the corpse, strange pinching tools clutched in one hand and a rattling bag in the other.

"It is ungodly to desecrate the dead," the princess said, despite the heartbeat of pain running from her leg to her throat.

"The dead don't need their teeth." The witch stood, brushing off her skirts. "And the eyetooth of one killed in violence can be used as a charm against drowning."

"That is ridiculous."

"Not if a sailor believes it." The witch looked at the princess then, bird-black eyes narrowed in suspicion.

At last, the princess thought, and then felt alarmed. Those words meant nothing. She had been waiting for nothing.

"The battlefield is no place for a woman," the princess said, because that was what a true knight would say.

"I am ministering to the wounded."

"You are mutilating corpses."

"Bit of both, then." The witch came closer. "I tell it true, m'lord. That wound will fester if not tended. I've seen men lose their legs to shallower cuts."

"I have bound it. I can see to it myself."

"Aye, bound it in your own rags, you have. In a fortnight, it will be black and you'll be begging for your friends to take a blade to it." The witch knelt suddenly, digging her hands into the soil. After a moment, she rose again, thin fingers clutching damp, gray earth.

"Beggar's clay," the witch said, meeting the princess's eye. "It will draw the sickness out."

"I have no need of your black magic." The thought of those hands against her skin made the princess feel nauseous. She hunched her shoulders, ready to be sick, but there was no food in her belly. She sank to her knees and heaved, dryly. The ground was spinning again, and the princess lay down on her back, squeezing her eyes shut. When she opened them, the witch was peering down at her.

"Lie still, for I do not wish to cut you." With a flash of silver, the witch sliced through the meager bandage with her dagger. The princess flinched, trying to force the other woman away.

"Lie still, I said," the witch hissed, spitting into her hand before smearing the clay mixture against the princess's thigh. The relief was immediate, and the princess almost let out a gasp in her true voice, a breathy female gasp that would have revealed her immediately.

Luckily, she composed herself in time. She had been playing this role for too long to let a kohl-eyed crone unmask her now.

"There now," the witch murmured. "Bind soft cotton over the clay, and change it nightly. In two days' time, the pain will ebb. In a moon, the scar will fade."

"Away from me, madwoman." The princess scrambled backward, putting distance between them. The witch still knelt before her, eyes wide and curious.

"As skittish as a colt, you are. And no more than a lad, I'd bet my throwing stones on it. I've never seen a grown man with eyes so blue."

The princess cast her blue eyes toward the ground. Many knights had thought her a boy before this; it was as good a disguise as any. Still, she remembered the witch's rough hand on her thigh, and felt a tremor run through her. It might have been fear, but it did not feel like fear.

"Fare thee well, then, my errant knight." The witch rose, wiping her clay-covered hands on her skirt. She tossed a look over her shoulder as she strode off into the smoke, and the princess watched the corner of her mouth curl, like the whorls of black ink marking her forearms.

'An ill omen, she is,' the princess thought, and her thoughts had the same low pitch as her voice these past few weeks. Already she was forgetting what she truly sounded like. Or perhaps she'd always sounded like this—gravel throated and weary. Perhaps this life was her truth now, and the other was nothing but a dream. A fairy tale.

They went to meet the enemy along the southern border, ten days' ride from the carnage of that first battle. The princess waited for dark magic to sweep like fever through the camp, but so far their strength had held.

"No thanks to her," the knights whispered, sneering toward the woodwitch who followed behind them. At night they burned sweetgrass and wild sage as offerings to their king. The princess hung back, offerings unlit. She knew, with a certainty cold as iron, that her father wanted none of her prayers. Since she had run, there had been no news from the palace of a missing princess. Perhaps he was keeping her secret safe, protecting her in what small way he could. Perhaps he had given her up completely.

In the trembling fire of offerings, the princess caught sight of a familiar, flame-limned profile. The witch sat at the edge of their party, shoulders drawn together against the cold. Already, the princess's leg had begun to itch with healing, the skin no longer swollen and pink. She often found herself looking to catch the woodwitch's eye, hoping to offer a nod of gratitude, an acknowledgment of her service. The witch never looked at her, however, and the princess had to content herself with indirect angles: the heavy slope of her brow, the elegant hook of her nose. She was indeed a witch of songs and stories, though she had no warts to speak of, and could not have been much older than the princess herself. Still, there was something about her to make children quake in their beds. Or at least something to make the princess quake, lying frantic and awake in her windblown cloth tent, aching for a blade to hold.

"The errant knight." The witch laughed low like music as the princess rode up beside her. "I did wonder how you fared."

"Not dead yet," the princess said, tangled in that laugh as if it were a web.

"As I see." Even as she said it, the witch did not look at her. "And your injury?"

"Healing well." The princess blushed even as she thought the words, but forced them through her teeth. "Thanks to you."

"Thanks indeed. Would that your company shared your gratitude."

The princess forced herself to look the witch full in the face, searching for any sign of cruelty. Her heart stuttered in her chest as if she were cutting throats; if anyone had hurt this woman, the princess did not know what she would do.

"What happened?" she snarled, teeth catching on her lips, "Who was it? Tell me his name and I'll...I'll..."

"You'll fight an army, will you?" The witch laughed again, though there was no longer music in it. "Never fear, lad. I can handle myself with a dagger."

The princess had slowed her horse to keep pace beside the

woman. She could feel him trembling between her legs with the
urge to run, and she petted his neck. They'd been together since
she took him from her father's stables with promises of oats and
sugar.

"A fine beast," the witch said, reaching up to trace her
fingers through the horse's chestnut mane. "Wherever did you
find him?"

"He was my father's," the princess said, a lie she had told
countless times. "A farmer, he was."

"How came a farmer's son to this endless war?"

"I wished to serve my king and vanquish his enemies."

The witch was silent for a moment, looking away with a
wry twist of her lips. "And what does a farmer's son know of
enemies?"

This was a conversation the princess had had before. She
knew her lines very well.

"The Raven's Gate is ours by right. Those lands belonged to
our ancient kings, not the godless men that claim them now."

"Are you so sure of this?" the witch asked. "I have heard
legend that the Gate belonged to the Green Men of the South
since time began."

"Those are the legends of Green Men."

"And your legends are your own." The witch brushed a thick
lock of hair from her eyes. The princess watched it slide through
her hand. "Who can say where the truth lies?"

The princess had no response. Such talk was treasonous, and
likely to get a man's throat cut.

"The South is building a great weapon with which they mean
to take our lands from us." That was a safer subject than the ambi-
guity of history. The threat from the South had been common
knowledge since the princess was a child. Mothers warned their
sons against Southern traders; rangers at the borders lit lanterns
through the night to keep unseen enemies at bay.

"What shape does this great weapon take? Or have you not seen it?" The witch kept her voice low.

"Of course I haven't. But there have been spies, scouts—"

"Who have spoken to you?"

"No, but who have spoken to our...commanding officers. Our king."

"Ah." The witch nodded. "And they would have no cause to lie."

No cause but the Raven's Gate, the princess thought, the mountain range said to be rich with minerals, and easy access to trade routes with the Islands. But surely—surely her father would not have spent so many lives for such a cause. Blood right, honor, certainly, but not gold.

"The South cast spells on our men, and killed the princes," the princess said, counting her brothers' names silently in her head: Nathyn, shy, fond of science and math and stray dogs. Elias, the archer, beloved by princesses and peasant women alike. Bertrand, strong and tall and thirsty for blood. Leif, the youngest and the sweetest, who gave her hand a kiss as he rode past her window on his way to war.

"Pray for me, sister," he called up to her, "I shall see you again before the lilacs bloom."

Leif, who had taught her how to swing a sword, taught her where to cut a man if you meant to kill him. Leif, two years her elder, who had curled up in her bed at night when thunder roared like a wounded beast. The enemy had killed him, and all her brothers before.

"Spells? What spells do you speak of, boy?" The witch interrupted the princess's thoughts.

"The fever that overran the army, five years ago. The flux that killed the youngest prince."

"Mercy." The witch touched her green hand to her heart, then to her lips. The princess followed that motion with her eyes—wordless, helpless. "The flux was the result of tainted rations. That meat was old and rotten, and the commanders knew it full well. If you would blame anyone for that, blame your king."

"Those words are treasonous," the princess spat, turning her horse to face the witch. The witch stopped in her tracks, but she did not bow her head. Instead, she met the princess's eyes with her own—not bird-black at all, but chocolate brown. In this light, the princess could finally see them clearly.

"Treasonous to whom?" the witch asked. "I should know the truth of it, I was there as those boys died."

"You were—"

"Don't look so surprised. I've been following armies and healing men longer than you've been a soldier."

"And yet you could not heal a dying prince."

The witch frowned, drawing her thick eyebrows together. "There were many men I could not heal, too many to count on fifty hands. Was this prince blond haired and green eyed? Was he gentle, with freckles on his cheekbones?"

"He—" the princess started and then stopped, choking the words back. "I do not know. I've only heard stories of his death."

"Pity," the witch murmured, "It is always a pity when gentle men die."

The princess dug her heels into her horse, and rode away. She did not look back at the witch, and she knew the witch did not look after her.

Two days away from the southern border, the army came across a slow-moving river. The men held their supplies over their heads, wading through the water with their horses behind them. Some of the younger ones went back to help the camp followers cross, carrying wee babes in their arms and old women on their shoulders. The sun was out, and when they had cleared the far banks, the army rested for a while at the forest's edge, as if war was nothing more than a bad dream on a beautiful day.

Men dove into the clear water to wash away the worst of the week's dust, and the princess watched their easy nakedness with envy. She had seen so much of male bodies that their shape held no mystery for her, nor much interest. She only wished that she might bathe as openly, instead of stealing into the woods at night, scrubbing herself in icy streams or tepid ponds. She wandered the edge of the river now, sweat beading beneath her leathers, wishing she might strip and disappear beneath the gentle waves.

When she had walked a fair distance, the shouts and laughter of the men fading away behind her, something dark broke the surface of the water. The princess started as the witch emerged with her head tossed back, gasping for breath.

"My errant knight," she said, blinking droplets of water from her eyelashes. "And here I thought I might sneak away unnoticed."

"I do not wish to intrude." The princess found her gaze drawn unwillingly to the witch's bare shoulders, just visible above the water. "I shall leave you to the river."

"Not one for swimming yourself?" the witch called out, even as the princess made to turn away.

"No, I...never learned." This lie had worked with the men, and though she earned a fair amount of teasing, it meant that she could keep her clothing on.

"I can teach you, if you like," the witch said, swimming closer. Her collarbones gleamed. "I was raised on the banks of the Western Sea. They say children there learn to swim before they learn to walk."

The princess could not picture the witch as a small child in a common fishing village. She could not imagine her as anything other than this woman in the water, drawing ever nearer like a predatory mermaid. It made the princess take a nervous step back.

"I rather prefer the land, thank you." The princess looked down the banks to where some of the soldiers had climbed out of the water, buckling into their mail and armor. "I think we are nearly on the move again as well."

"Such a shame," the witch said. "There is nothing so refreshing as a swim."

With that, she walked calmly to the shore and stepped up onto the bank.

For a moment, the princess was so shocked that she could not look away. Water ran in rivulets between the witch's full, dark-nippled breasts, over her curving stomach and ample thighs. Between her legs there was a thatch of thick black hair, glistening with water like a scattering of jewels. The princess realized that this was the only female body she'd ever seen, save her own. Did all other women look like this—as round and soft as sweet fruit ripened by the sun? More strange tattoos covered the witch's legs, and the princess felt her lips part, wondering what those tattoos might feel like beneath her hands. Was the skin raised, or was it soft, or...

"Your face is red, my lad," the witch said, stepping closer. The princess quickly turned her head but not before she caught sight of the witch's breasts again, nipples hardened like black cherries. "Too much sun, perhaps."

"You should exercise more modesty in the company of men," the princess said, fumbling for words she imagined an earnest man might say, a man whose pulse was not fluttering like the wings of a moth. "Think of your virtue—"

"My virtue." The witch laughed. "Yes, think of that."

She was so close that the princess could smell her, and she smelled like smoke and soil and the river. The princess closed her eyes as the witch leaned forward, brushing a damp kiss against her cheek. Then the witch laughed again and walked away, hair spilling like ink down her back. The princess kept her eyes on the river. There was an ache inside her she had never felt before, radiating out from the wound on her leg, where rough hands had once smoothed cold clay.

That night, alone in her tent, she did not yearn for blades or weapons. She did not know the words for what she wanted.

The next battle was worse than the last. The princess lost count of the number of men she wiped off the edge of her sword. A particularly vicious soldier even attacked her horse, and the princess took his head off before he could do much more than scratch the beast. Still, the horse's cries were terrible to hear. The princess got to her knees on the forest floor until she found that same gray clay, smearing it across the animal's bleeding ribs. That seemed to calm him, and she rode through the aftermath, seeking out men in need of help, or men who were too slow in their dying. She saw the witch from a distance, burning sweet-grass at the feet of a crumpled body, performing her strange green-fisted ritual. The princess also saw the enemy soldier stag-gering to his feet behind the witch's back, picking himself up with ruined hands and raising his dagger.

She was across the clearing in an instant, sword cutting the man down before he could take more than a step in the witch's direction. The witch turned her head just in time to see the soldier bleed and fall, but the look she leveled at the princess was not grateful.

"The battlefield is no place for a woman," the princess said, voice unsteady with fear and relief. Her sword was dripping scarlet.

"Nor for children," the witch said, gesturing to the body over which she prayed. The princess had to cover her mouth with her hand. The boy was wearing armor, and the bright

colors of their king, but he could not have been older than thir-
teen. How had such a child found his way into the army? The
princess did not recognize him, but she felt like she should. She
felt like she should have seen him and sent him home, where
children belonged.

"I am sick to death of this war," the witch said.

The princess leaned forward, offering her hand. She wanted
to put the witch on her horse and take her far from the meat of
the battle, take her somewhere where she might be safe.

But the witch shook her head. She looked away, returning to
her prayers over boys that should not need them.

The princess rode away alone.

That night, the princess woke to find someone in her tent.
She was sitting up and reaching for her dagger before her eyes
adjusted to the dim firelight coming through the canvas. It only
took a moment to recognize the figure crawling toward her,
eyes wide and lambent as the moon. She was dreaming, she told
herself, because she had had this dream before.

"What are you…"

"I cannot sleep while you lie alone in this tent," the witch
murmured, climbing boldly into her lap. "You are keeping me
awake."

She threaded her fingers behind the princess's neck and
leaned down, placing a biting kiss along her jawline. The princess gasped with shock, hands rising to the witch's waist to push
her away. Strangely enough, they held her in place.

"Yes, there." The witch bit the other side of her neck, tracing
the pain away with her tongue.

"I do not know how to…I've never…"

"I'll show you," the witch said, breath hot on the princess's
skin.

She took one of the princess's hands and suckled at the

fingers, a long slow slide of lips that made the princess cry out. The noise would not be contained no matter how she tried, and she heard some of the men chuckle around the campfire outside.

"Lift my skirts," the witch told her, unashamed, and the princess did. She rucked up the heavy layers of wool, sliding her wet-fingered hand underneath and finding warm, bare thighs. Her hand traveled up those thighs of its own volition, and soon there was coarse and tangled hair against her fingertips. She had seen that hair when the witch stepped naked out of the river, and the thought of that moment made the princess cry out again.

"Inside," the witch said, hips jerking slightly. "Put them inside."

The princess pushed inward, finding warmth and wetness. She knew what men and women did together, and she knew what they did alone. There was a great difference between knowing, however, and feeling someone else's pulse around your fingertips, sliding deeper and deeper until a dark-haired woman threw her head back and moaned brokenly.

Someone whistled outside the tent, but the witch did not seem to hear them. She clenched her thighs, raising and lowering herself over the princess's fingers, and the princess felt something flare low in her stomach, a want so fierce it was almost pain.

"That's a good lad," the witch gasped. "There, yes, there."

The princess wished to touch herself, but she wanted to touch the witch more. Her free hand tugged at the laces of the woman's bodice until one breast spilled out, and she cradled it in her palm. The nipple was large and soft and dark, and when the princess grasped it, the witch gave a panicked little cry.

"Harder," she said, and the princess squeezed her harder, the way she wanted to do on the banks of the river, her hands ravenous.

The witch leaned forward then, pressing their mouths together. The sensation was alien and yet so familiar, and when the witch licked her tongue into the princess's mouth, the whole world went white-hot as a star. A cry was building low in the witch's throat, the princess could feel it humming against her mouth, but it grew and grew until the witch turned her head and wailed, hips rocking, hands clenching on the princess's shoulders. There was more laughter from the world outside the tent, but the princess barely took notice. The witch was kissing her slow and deep, her body pliant. When she pulled back, their eyes locked, and the princess saw shadows of a young girl from a fishing village, and a woman wet from a river, and magic both light and dark.

The witch put her hands on the princess's shoulders, pushing her gently down until she lay flat on her back. She crawled forward then, spreading her skirts and her legs until she strad-dled the princess's face, and the princess found her mouth full of wet flesh and salt-sweet hair. Skirts fell on every side of her, blocking out the light.

"Again," the witch said. The princess parted her lips and tasted.

That night the witch showed the princess how to use her fingers and her mouth, how to touch her above and below to make her writhe with fearsome pleasure. The witch rode her tongue and her fingers and her thigh and her fist—pushing her down, pulling her hair, taking her again and again. As dawn approached, the princess found hands on the lacings of her tunic and the ties of her leggings and she was so exhausted and trans-fixed that she didn't resist until it was almost too late.

"You must not," she whispered. "There is something I have not—you do not know—"

"Hush love." The witch arranged the princess on her hands and knees, kissing down her back. "Let me tell you a story."

The princess tried to protest, but was shocked silent by the feeling of a hand on her bare stomach, traveling toward her ribs. It seemed a lifetime since she had been touched.

"Once upon a time, a daughter was born to a great king," the witch whispered, pushing the princess's tunic up across her back. The princess heard the words from a great distance, weightless and reborn. "This princess was tall and strong, and could wield a sword more skillfully by ten than many men by twenty." The witch's hand reached the binding keeping the princess's breasts flat, but the princess barely noticed. The witch unfastened it with one hand, loosening the material until it slid to the ground. When she took one of the small breasts in her warm palm, the princess arched her back and nearly wept. It was if she had been dying of thirst since the moment she laid eyes on this woman, and was finally being offered wine.

"She had a strong jaw and a sweet voice." The witch lowered her hands to the princess's hips, easing her leggings down. "And when her father had no more sons to offer up in battle, the princess cut her flaxen hair and rode to fight for her kingdom." The witch rolled the princess's leggings over her thighs to her knees, gently guiding one leg free and then another. The princess felt as if she were watching someone else's life, someone else's naked body kneeling in a tiny tent, with a dark-haired woman crouched behind them. Her hips were jerking unthinkingly, knees trembling. No one had ever—she had never—

"Oh, please."

"Of course, it is just a story," the witch whispered, hands sliding between the princess's shaking thighs. "But I would so love to meet a princess such as that. How...remarkable she must be."

The witch knelt down and spread the princess's legs. She pressed her mouth between them, and the princess was lost.

* * *

Grave news was carried on the morning wind, spreading across the kingdom like dry leaves. The king had sent messengers to every battalion with news to make a grown man weep: the princess, his only daughter, had been murdered by the enemy while she slept. Her body had been defiled in such a way that it was nigh unrecognizable, and the king burned the corpse in despair. He only hoped that this tragedy would inspire his armies to fight even more fiercely for their kingdom. The destruction of their enemies to the south was all that could bring the princess peace.

The soldiers wailed and cursed while the message was read aloud, swearing vengeance in one breath and murder in the next. Astride her horse, thighs still loose and aching, the princess wiped away a single tear. Then she pulled on the reins and turned her horse around.

It took no time at all to find her; the witch stood out like a smudge of black ink on clean parchment. The princess brought the horse up alongside her, but the witch kept her gaze straight ahead.

"Tragic news," she murmured.

"I am sick to death of this war," the princess replied, uncaring who heard.

This earned a sharp glance from her dark-eyed love. Love, yes—that was the word for it. The princess had finally found the words for what she wanted.

"As are we all," the witch said. "If only there was someone who might speak against it. Someone the kingdom might heed."

The princess rode beside her in silence for a moment, considering this.

"There is a rumor that my family is cursed," she said. "That none of my line will ever ride away from battle."

She stopped her horse, and leaned down. She offered the witch her hand.

The witch smiled.

Swinging her up into the saddle was as easy as breathing. Easier. The witch wrapped her arms around the princess's waist, and the princess broke a curse.

# THE PRIZE OF
# THE WILLOW

## H. N. Janzen

There was once a couple who went to live on a small farm where there had been a great fire a hundred years before their time. Though the farm was far from any towns or settlements, the man had inherited it from his uncle, and both he and his wife being the youngest children in large families, they had moved to the remote place in the hope that they could make a better living than they might have at home.

As they traveled through the young woods between the last road and the house, the woman became quite tired, and they sat down to rest by a creek in the very center of the budding forest. She lay beside it for a spell, and as the early spring sun in the leaves lit up her hair, her husband was struck anew by her beauty. Though they had been married fifteen years, they had never had any children, and it was without any concern for the possibility of conception that they enjoyed each other. Sure enough, though, by the end of the winter, a baby girl was born to the couple. Her name was Agatha, and she was good.

Agatha grew to be strong and tall, with skin as tan as an

acorn and long blonde tresses that she kept tied back in a braid. Her hands were rough from long hours of work, but her eyes sparkled with the curiosity and wonder of a girl half her age. She cared for the animals, threw herself into tending the crops, and had never been tempted to leave the farm by the visits they made to town to sell their harvest and buy what they could not produce.

Despite herself, though, it was the growing woods that held the most allure for Agatha. Every year, the new trees grew tall and strong as she did, and every year, when she could, she would remain out amongst them late into the night. Her parents warned her against these journeys, telling her tales of bandits and beasts, but when she was sixteen, her mother passed away, and by the time she was eighteen, Agatha tended the farm alone.

One warm summer night, after she had finished in the fields, Agatha decided that she had time to wander the woods. Past the birch with the crow's nest and through the shortawn meadow foxtails grew what Agatha estimated to be the oldest tree in the forest. The weeping willow sat in the center, long branches hanging like a veil. On the edge of its perimeter was a large rock that stretched from the earth like a giant's thumb, and it was behind this that Agatha was seated when she saw the dryad.

First a foot emerged, then a leg, then hips. A woman's hips. Agatha was transfixed as the dryad materialized out of the tree as easily as if she were stepping through a waterfall. Her skin was a deep brown, like the bark, but as smooth as a petal, and instead of hair, she had long, hanging branches just like the willow itself. As she lit on the roots of the tree, her full breasts bounced, and Agatha felt something stir within her that had never awoken before. She gasped, the sensation searing her, and immediately the dryad turned to the rock. Before Agatha could react, the dryad had closed the distance between them. The moment her eyes set on Agatha, she drew back.

"Wait!" Agatha cried out.

The dryad paused.

"My parents told me stories of the fair folk. By what manner do I keep your company? Is there a riddle or a quest? I will do whatever it takes, for I am all alone on my farm," Agatha said.

The dryad stepped back tentatively.

"You are all alone?" she asked.

Agatha nodded.

The dryad smiled. "I am also alone," she said.

The dryad claimed to not have a name, so Agatha called her Willow. She said that she did not remember the fire, but it had devastated the forest, killing the previous dryad and leaving only a handful of sprouting trees alive. As such, Willow, too, was alone. All she had learned about herself and her situation, she had learned from a nymph passing along the small creek that flowed through the copse. The nymph had advised her to avoid the violent humans, too, but like Agatha, she was lonely, young, and eager. Against any reservations she may have had, Willow agreed to see Agatha again, then again, and by the end of summer, Agatha had worn a path to her favorite tree in the middle of the woods.

Willow asked the question when the air had just ripened with the sweet, full smell of autumn. She and Agatha both sat with their feet in the creek, for Agatha's were tired after her day in the field. As they conversed, Agatha gradually removed all of her garments until she was naked as a forest animal. Willow's eyes strayed in fascination at the similarities between them whenever Agatha turned away, and finally, when Agatha lay back on the moss, Willow could not remain reserved any longer.

"Agatha, does humankind do as the other animals do in the springtime?"

Agatha sat up. "Pardon?"

Willow shifted on the rocks, and the moss grew further to cushion her. "To make young," she said.

For a moment, Agatha was startled. This was a topic her parents had told her about in detail so that she could not be fooled by anyone who might try to prey on her innocence in town. "Yes," she said finally, "but we do not always do it to make young."

Willow's leaves perked up with confusion. "Why else would you suffer a man?"

Agatha searched the dryad's face. "I would not suffer a man," she admitted. "But some women find it pleasurable."

"What could be pleasurable about it?" Willow asked.

Agatha's heart sped up. Slowly, so that Willow might pull away if she wished, Agatha put her right hand on Willow's jaw and leaned forward. Tenderly, almost chastely, Agatha pressed her red lips to Willow's deep brown ones and kissed. Only the hot breath that ghosted across Willow's mouth before Agatha pulled away indicated that the touch had been one of desire and not tutorial.

Willow looked at her with shining eyes. "Oh," she said.

This time, Willow met Agatha in the middle, and Agatha wrapped her in her strong arms. When they broke apart for breath, Agatha put her index finger on Willow's chin and held her mouth open, then licked her bottom lip. Willow reached her tongue out, too, and for a moment, they touched, tentatively, before Agatha pushed forward and probed Willow's mouth, brushing the roof, then tangling tongues again. Willow's breath was like clover after the rain, and Agatha's free hand wrapped itself in Willow's branches, pulling her closer so that she could probe deeper. This time, when they separated, she found that Willow's hands had also been busy. Cascading around her face and down her shoulders, Agatha's blonde hair fell free from its usual braid.

"That is what the humans do?" Willow asked.

"That is only the beginning," Agatha said.

Willow put her chin to her collarbone and looked up at Agatha from below her brows. "Would you show me more?"

Agatha smiled. This time, she shared another soft kiss with Willow, then began kissing her way down her neck and continued on until she reached Willow's breasts. They were heavy and plush, bountiful as nature itself, and topped with nipples the color of rich mahogany. Though Willow was of the woods, her body was pliant and supple.

Agatha had never engaged in these activities with anyone else before, but she thought of what felt good on her many lonely nights, and she brushed her thumb against one of Willow's nipples. When the dryad gasped, Agatha gained confidence and decided to experiment. Using her left hand to tweak Willow's right breast, Agatha dipped her head and licked the other nipple, then took it in her mouth and sucked on it. This time, Willow arched her back.

"Oh, Agatha!" she mewled.

As Agatha continued her ministrations, Willow put one hand on her shoulder, gripping her tightly, and with the other, she reached for Agatha's chest. Her breasts were pert, small, and firm, and Willow took one into her hand entirely, massaging it and occasionally pinching Agatha's nipple in between her fore- and middle-finger. The first time that she did this, Agatha whimpered, and the second time, she began to feel that tingling in her groin that said she could wait no longer.

Willow groaned when Agatha stopped suckling, but the farmer stroked down her spine, gently laying her on the moss.

"I will show you the most pleasurable part of all," Agatha said.

Trailing kisses, Agatha worked her way downward, tasting Willow's soft skin. She used an arm to position one of Willow's thighs over her shoulder, and with the other hand she stroked the inside of Willow's other leg, moving her hand tantalizingly close, then back down.

Though Willow was always nude, Agatha had only caught the barest glimpse of what lay between the dryad's legs, and now, with everything on full display, she felt another powerful swell of arousal. Like the inside of a healthy tree, Willow's inner lips were dewy and a pale green. Agatha lightly trailed her middle finger over the clitoral hood and down one side of her nether lips. Reflexively, Willow bucked up, moaning. With the arm wrapped around Willow's thigh, Agatha used the less calloused pad of her thumb to rub Willow's clit, and with the other, she continued lightly tracing her nethers, teasing the entrance to Willow's body, but never pushing in.

For a few minutes, Willow reclined and let the feelings flow through her, strange but wonderful, just like Agatha herself was. But eventually, before she was truly lost in the sensation, she pulled away, and Agatha's head shot up, questioning.

"Kneel over me, please. I want to touch you," Willow begged.

Agatha grinned. Placing her legs on either side of Willow's head, she returned to her ministrations from a new, top-down angle. Willow, meanwhile, took a moment to enjoy the sight of Agatha on display for her. Agatha's skin beneath her clothes was pale, but here, her skin was flushed scarlet and lightly carpeted in blonde curls. Willow touched with her thumb, mimicking Agatha's movements, and this time, it was Agatha's turn to mewl. She was soaking wet, and Willow could smell her heady scent. Impulsively, she pulled Agatha's taut rump down toward her face and licked at the source of the smell. This elicited a louder moan than anything else, so she did it again, with the same result. The taste was bitter, and like nothing Willow had ever eaten before. She liked it.

Agatha, feeling how good Willow's tongue felt, could not deny her the same pleasure. As she felt her own nethers being bathed, she lapped Willow's clit as well. The dryad squealed and bucked into her face. Using her now free hand, she held Willow's hips down and began to work herself into a rhythm, enjoying the syrupy taste. When she found exactly what motion would elicit the loudest response, she kept at it, making circles around Willow's button, while Willow moved her tongue vertically for Agatha.

Willow's orgasm was sudden and powerful. With short, jagged thrusts, she finished, and it was all Agatha could do to keep her in place while she continued licking, occasionally dipping her head to catch the juices pushed out by the force of Willow's spasms. Feeling Willow against her whole body and feeling the muscle contractions through her arm, Agatha could hold back no longer, and as Willow's orgasm subsided, Agatha reached her own completion. Willow gladly lapped at the heat of Agatha's sex, even as Agatha sat back onto her face, unable to stay upright as she gasped and groaned.

When Agatha was done, she sat up, then lay beside Willow on the moss, pulling the dryad into her arms. In this fashion they rested for a time, listening to the sounds of the forest and enjoying the twinges still running through them. Finally, though, Willow sat up.

"You must go," she said. "It will be dark soon."

"You should come with me to the farmhouse. It may be small, but the bed is big enough for both of us," Agatha urged.

Willow began to braid Agatha's hair again. "I cannot stray that far from the trees. Where the forest does not reach, I cannot go," she said.

Agatha nodded slowly, already considering the solution. "Would you come, if you could?" she asked.

The look Willow gave her was almost teary. "I want nothing more," she said.

Resolution filled Agatha. "Then you will someday," she promised, and stood up.

For the rest of that autumn, Willow came to the edge of the forest once her own curation of the woods was complete to watch Agatha in the fields every day. Though Agatha made her own breakfasts, bread and cheese, Willow brought her fruits, roots, and nuts from the forest for lunch and supper. Agatha harvested alone, but the presence of her favorite onlooker galvanized her. With supper waiting for her, and dessert even more enticing, Agatha was happy to work as hard as she possibly could.

With the onset of the winter, though, Willow came to Agatha full of sorrow. "I must hibernate with the trees," she said. "Though I need little sleep year-round, in the winter, I incubate in the willow."

Agatha felt her heart sink. "I will be thinking of nothing else but your return all winter," she said, blinking rapidly. "Is there anything I can set myself to in order to ease your awakening?"

Willow thought for a moment. "I am always freezing cold when I rise from my slumber. The summer is warm, but the spring is cold for many weeks."

"I will make you a woolen blanket," Agatha promised.

Sure enough, the next spring, when Willow smelled the rain on the forest air and was called back to the woods, she found a new woolen blanket wrapped around the tree. Bunching it around herself, she ran to the edge of the woods, the snow unpleasant on her feet even if it would not harm her. When she reached the edge, she could see that it was early morning, the sky purple and gold in successive layers.

"Agatha!" she shouted.

In less than a minute, someone stumbled out of the house, shielded their eyes from the sun, then ran across the fields. "Willow!" Agatha yelled back.

Willow caught Agatha in her arms and began to kiss her. Agatha kissed back, then pulled away. "Come," she said. "It is warmer inside."

"Inside?" Willow asked, puzzled.

Agatha took her by the hand and led her halfway around the field. As they approached, Willow could see what appeared to be the bare structure of a fence, but as they got closer, she realized what she was truly seeing.

"You planted trees across the field?"

"They already grow around the house for shade. You can come inside now. You may wake up cold, but you can come into the warmth whenever you please," Agatha said.

Willow could see the furrows where the frost had been doggedly chipped through so that the reedy saplings could be replanted. As Agatha led her down the row, she stared in wonder at the small, hunched cabin, surrounded by trees just as Agatha had said. Up close, she could smell the wood smoke, and she froze.

"Your home is on fire!" she said.

Agatha stopped. "It is only the fireplace. You will be safe."

Willow stared back at her, hope and fear wrestling for dominance.

Agatha went back and pulled Willow close to her. "When I am forced to make a journey to town, I meet women who are trapped by their duties and the places they live. I saw their lives and I thought that to share my life with another would be to lose my freedom to explore and be the mistress of my own domain. Now that I know you, Willow, I realize that I was wrong. I see you bid the plants to grow, and I know that I have found someone who is as much a mistress of her domain as I am the mistress of mine. I love your lonely heart, your protective soul, and your adventurous spirit. Willow...I love you."

Willow smiled a great smile then, one as radiant as the

sunrise. Stooping down, Agatha scooped her up and carried Willow into the house. She did not stop until she reached the bedroom, and there they remained until the sun was well over the fields.

For many years, Agatha and Willow had great happiness. Willow would help in the fields sometimes, and when she could, Agatha would help in the forest as well.

Willow became accustomed to being in the house, and Agatha was never bothered by the larger animals in the forest thanks to Willow's intervention. Using her knowledge of farming, Agatha did her best to enhance the growth of Willow's tree, and every few winters, she would need to knit a new blanket for Willow's awakening.

Willow grew taller, and her face became that of a woman, not a girl. As time passed, however, Agatha grew stronger, then smarter, and then suddenly more frail. Willow watched in consternation as Agatha's blonde hair faded to white and her once-toned frame became thin. More and more, she focused her energies on the fields, growing Agatha the food she would need for the winter, since Willow could not provide for her then and Agatha could not do it on her own.

One fall, as the first tendrils of frost snaked over the morning grass, Agatha measured the oldest tree in the forest, now nearly two centuries old, and found it already much larger around the middle than the year previous. Her face split into a grin.

"I have to knit another one," she said.

"Please, save your strength," Willow begged. "I will run to the house when I awaken."

"You will be cold," Agatha said, "and I must have some way to distract myself from missing you."

That night, they made love tenderly, but with the skill of two people who have mastered the art of the other person's body. In the morning, shivering beneath her cloak but too stubborn to admit it, Agatha walked with Willow back to the tree and watched as her lifelong companion entered it in the same effortless way she had once stepped out of it so many years ago. Then she returned to the farmhouse and pulled out the wool.

The winter was long and hard that year, and nearing the end, Agatha found that she did not have enough food to last her. Taking some of the old blankets that were now too small for the willow, she hobbled out into the snow and began her journey to the town. She made it by nightfall, and managed to trade the blankets for enough food to last her if she was careful. However, without any money, she could not stay at an inn for the night, and so it was that she began her trip home in the dark.

After all these years, Agatha was hardly surprised when she was waylaid on the roadside. Stubborn and still strong at heart, she refused to hand over her food. They left her with broken bones and a bleeding scalp, laughing at the foolish pride of an old woman, and took even her cloak. At first, she thought she might mend if she made it home, but as the night wore on, Agatha realized that this would likely be her last. Then, she considered, why not wait peacefully for death to come? But even as she considered resting her cracked hip, she caught a hint of warmth and rain in the night, and she knew she had to press on.

The morning sun was high when Agatha finally limped through the doorway of her home. Though she felt the chill deep in her bones, she did not tarry long. She was soon out the door, and then into the woods for the last time. Agatha knew that without her to tend the tree as only a farmer could, that old willow might not grow as fast as it had up until now. She had to make sure that her last contribution was nourishing. As best she could, Agatha wrapped the new blanket around the tree and kissed her willow for the last time.

To this day, some say that if you can find the town, you can find the old forest that burned down long ago. At the very center of those woods is a willow tree with the very tattered, very old remains of a woolen blanket around it. If you can do this, and you know what to look for, then you can still see the remains of a skeleton held fast in the roots, too closely to ever remove without killing the tree.

# TOADS, DIAMONDS, AND THE OCCASIONAL PEARL

## Emily L. Byrne

All the stories begin the same way: three princes go on a quest. Maybe they're rivals for a throne. Or a princess. But whatever the goal, the youngest one always wins. Unless it's the eldest. They never have sisters. Or if they do, they're left safely at home.

When I told my father, the king, that I wanted to go on a quest like my two brothers had, he laughed. He made my request a joke, as if he had not known that I practiced all that my brothers learned from the armsmaster since we were small. Perhaps I had kept that secret too well.

The whole court buzzed with the news of my humiliation, except for my younger brother, Fenar. He longed for the peace of the library and the quiet of the monastery. And that was where I parted from him when I left our father's castle, taking his sword, his horse, and his name with his blessing.

Our father had forbidden me all three and I intended to prove him wrong. I could win the throne, if not the princess. Princess Eliann was lovely to look at, but she'd never glanced at me. Not since I kissed her once when I was on a visit to her mother's court and found myself barred from it until I "could learn to behave like a princess."

I sighed. When I saw Eliann next, we were both of marriageable age and things had changed. She was proud and cruel, no longer willing to meet my eyes, not even when I made my brothers stop teasing her. In any case, Eliann would never accept being consort to the Princess Shalene when she could be queen to my eldest brother, Greir, so my wishes were of little significance.

That was, of course, if Greir chose to claim her hand along with the throne when he returned. I thought it unlikely. Eliann's...affliction had put off braver men than he. Few would choose to be married to a princess who spat out diamonds or toads with every sentence. Mother had said that true love would break the fairy curse, but I had my doubts.

I shrugged off my thoughts, which made my horse snort at me and toss his head, eager to run. I felt the same way. Once I had seen other lands, I promised myself that I would find a princess and a throne of my own and never return here, just as my great aunt had done. The day turned brighter and my road clearer at that picture. I nudged the horse forward into a loping run and I smiled to think of leaving all I knew behind me.

I smiled less when I reached the edge of the great forest of Adin. The sun was setting and the figure on the path in front of me was in shadow, but I could still see the outline of a bow, its string stretched taut. The arrow was pointed straight at me. I pulled my horse to an abrupt halt. "I mean you no harm." I tried to make my voice as deep as my brother's.

The arrow stayed right where it was. "How do I know that?" It was odd, the quaver in that voice, almost like someone trying to sound older and larger than they were. I wondered if there were others on the road who traveled in disguise tonight. Did my brother's light armor make me so very terrifying?

Not that the arrow would make me less dead, terrifying or not. Something moved in the shadows at the figure's feet, but it was too small to be threatening. I hoped. I tried again, "I seek only to pass. Will you let me by?"

"Give me your horse." This time, I could hear the desperation in that voice. That, and something more. Something familiar. I wondered how well they could shoot, this person in shadow, who wanted to steal my horse. I wondered what I would do if they succeeded. I pictured my return to my father's court, my quest at an end, and me the utter failure they thought me already. A boiling rage filled me then. Kicking the horse forward into a full gallop while I drew my sword was a matter of pure impulse.

The arrow, when it flew, went wide. As did the horse as he dumped me unceremoniously on top of the archer in a sprawling mass of limbs and imprecations. Both bow and sword fell to the side as we wrestled, grappling for each other's throats, for an imagined weapon, for...the fading light of day fell on the archer's face. Princess Eliann scowled up at me, "You!"

A small toad leapt from her mouth and hopped off into the grass and she stopped looking at me and stared after it. Some things never changed. I contemplated rolling off her, then decided to stay where I was. Despite what I thought of Eliann's personality and...affliction, I could not deny that her personal endowments were unparalleled. Besides, sooner or later she had to notice me if I was sitting on top of her.

I spoke as coldly as I could manage, "I could say the same thing. How do you come to be playing the highwayman in the Adin Forest? I thought that you were waiting to find out which of my brothers would return to win your hand."

"Because naturally you're the only one who wants something else—" Princess Eliann pinched her full lips tightly closed and glared at me through narrowed gray eyes. In contrast to her olive complexion, they looked silver in the fading light, like small daggers. And if she could have stabbed me with her gaze alone, she would have done it.

It was probably past time for me to arise and catch my horse. I stood with a sigh, as much for my new bruises as for having to part company with Eliann's curves. But I remained as chivalrous as any knight and reached out my hand to help her up.

She accepted my assistance with an ill grace. "As if there was any question which of your brothers would succeed on a quest! Greir is far and away a better warrior than Fenar." She glanced up and down my armor and her eyes narrowed. "Isn't that Fenar's armor you're wearing? I remember it from when he rode out." Eliann's voice dropped as a thought occurred to her. "How...? You didn't kill him, did you?" Toads galore, followed by a small chunk of burnt metal of indefinable composition.

I burst out laughing and nudged a toad on its way before whistling for my horse the way Fenar had taught me. A moment later, there were hoofbeats on the road. "No. Why would I do that? He's my favorite. I left him at the monastery at Castlerock, happily reading his way through their library. He has no love for—" It was my turn to fall silent abruptly, remembering the company I now kept. Fenar loathed Eliann, but I could hardly say so to her.

Apparently, she heard what I didn't say. Eliann scuffed her foot in the dust of the road and looked down, her expression forlorn. "Me. I know. None of you do. But everyone wants my mother's domain. And my dowry. Even you are willing to pick up a sword for it." She tilted her face up to glare at me and spat out some creatures I couldn't identify in the growing dark, but which I hoped were still toads.

"Not me. I'm leaving the kingdom," I said, as matter-of-factly as I could. "I've realized that Father will give my hand to some lordling for a trade alliance without a thought to my happiness or lack thereof if I stay. I trained alongside my brothers, whether they knew it or not. Why should I do fewer deeds of valor than Greir?"

It was Eliann's turn to laugh. "Deeds of valor? You just fell off your horse on top of me!"

"I leapt," I declared coldly. And, lovely curves or no lovely curves, once my horse came back, he and I would be on our way again. I pretended that I no longer cared why Eliann was here, or for anything else about her. I only needed to find a campsite before night fell in earnest. Somewhere far away from toads and the faint scent of a smithy.

A roar from somewhere nearby shook the forest around us. Eliann's curves were molded to me, armor and all, an instant later. "Can you really use that sword?" she murmured into my shoulder, turning her face aside to daintily spit out what looked like a damp flower.

Fleeing Eliann was no longer my first plan. Instead, I picked up my sword before wrapping a cautious arm around her and pulling her closer. The warm press of her body against mine helped to soothe my otherwise trembling limbs as I stared into the trees over her head. Fenar's horse was galloping toward us as quickly as he had originally fled for the forest, and beautiful princess in my arms or not, I wanted to be on his back.

Nothing moved in the trees behind him so I risked another whistle. The horse's ears pricked and he slowed as he got closer to us. I released Eliann reluctantly and caught his trailing reins. "Perhaps we should go back to my father's castle?" A second roar, this one much closer, shook the ground around us. The horse broke free and fled, nearly dragging me with it.

Eliann scrambled around behind me, fumbling with her bow as I waved my sword in the general direction of the trees and tried to look menacing. "Shouldn't we just run? Maybe it won't be able to find us if we hide." She pointed south of the now-shifting trees on the road ahead of us. I grabbed her hand and we bolted, slinking down into the tall grass as best we could while we raced for the far edge of the forest.

Then we went sprawling on outstretched roots, smacked our faces into branches, and occasionally ran headlong into tree trunks in our flight. After the third such mishap, I slowed to rub my bruised face and listen for sounds of pursuit. But once I had waved Eliann into quieter panting, there was nothing except the usual woodsy sounds: sleepy birds, the distant crackling of leaves, and the babble of flowing water.

Eliann cocked her head to one side. Then she walked around us in a circle, alternately sniffing and listening. I wondered if her...affliction made her hear or smell better than I did. If so, at least the fairy who cursed her gave her that much. Well, that and the occasional gem to build her dowry. That was enough to make me consider my light money pouch; since fortune had thrown us together and Eliann spat out more gems when she was happy, perhaps I might find a way to make her so.

She pointed off into the trees and started walking. I followed her and hoped with all my heart that we were not walking toward the source of the roaring. But soon I was relieved that she was correct when we stumbled into a clearing with a brook running through it.

The pool that it emptied into was a few more steps away, as I discovered by nearly falling into it. Eliann caught my arm as I wavered on the edge of a small cliff. "You're sure about the whole deeds of valor thing? Maybe you should reconsider." The toad that popped out of her mouth looked perplexed but happy as it vanished into the pool below us.

I bit back a growl as another thought occurred to me. "Do you have any idea what comes out when?" I said, as casually as I could as we walked down to the edge of the pool. I looked around the clearing to avoid meeting Eliann's eyes. She never responded well to being asked about her…affliction. But nothing popped out of the trees except the moon, shining down to light our way.

When we were standing still and the silence had become deafening, I risked a sidelong glance at her. She was frowning, but at the water, not at me. Then at last, she sighed and glanced back at me. "It's a curse, so yes and no. If I'm really happy, it's often jewels. But sometimes, it's just happy toads. It's like it can't make up its mind."

"Why did the fairy curse you anyway? I thought the fairies usually gave minor blessings to royal infants. I got a blessing for excellent teeth and my brothers got bravery and wisdom and all that sort of thing." I found my excellent teeth clenching shut over a few expletives of my own. Why didn't I get bravery and wisdom, too? Stupid fairies.

Eliann gave me a considering look, as if she was wondering the same thing that I was. Then she looked away, her expression suggesting that there was more that she wasn't ready to say. "My mother offended one of the most powerful fairies. She said that she tried to apologize, but they cursed me anyway." She shrugged and spat out two small diamonds and what appeared to be a ruby.

After a moment, she continued, "I don't know whether or not I believe her. But at least the fairies gave me a way out: all I have to do to break the curse is to convince someone to fall in love with me." Her face lit up as though there was a candle behind it. A rose, perfect in its redness, dropped from her lips and I caught it before it could fall to the ground.

The light in Eliann's face dimmed and she grimaced. Then she handed me the jewels and the flower. I tucked the rose in my cloak and the jewels in my belt pouch. Perhaps we could trade them for food if we got tired of hunting.

When I looked back up, Eliann was rubbing at a deep scratch

on one shapely arm. "I want a bath," she said, her voice dreamy, as if her thoughts were somewhere else. She stretched and began removing her tunic. I started and gaped, valor and cleverness tossed aside much like Eliann's clothes. Her endowments were even more delightful when unfettered by the sort of clothing a disguised princess might wear. And before I was done admiring them, she pulled off her boots and breeches and jumped into the pool.

The wave she sent up splashed over me and soaked me to the skin. She laughed as she surfaced but her lips remained toad-free. That was enough to make me entertain a long-forgotten fantasy about what might have happened if her mother had not banned me from visiting them.

A light breeze caressed my wet clothes and brought me back to the present. From the expectant look on Eliann's face, I was clearly supposed to follow her example and join her in the water. But I hesitated. She already thought me a fool. What if she thought me an ugly one, too?

The moonlight glistened on her wet flesh as she swam and splashed and I ached to be close to her, to hold her in my arms. I sat down on the wet grass and took off my boots. My other clothes followed more slowly, at least until I considered that Greir would have already dived in.

There was something different about Eliann tonight, apart from her lack of clothes. Watching her splash merrily in the moonlit pool gave me a dull ache just below my belly that spread in waves of heat down my legs, then upward through the rest of my limbs. It was a strange new sensation that seemed to increase the longer I looked at her.

When she looked up and beckoned to me again, I did not deny her. Instead, I slid awkwardly out of the bindings that made me look more like a man when I rode alone. Looking down at myself, I could not help but think that I did not strip to advantage, not like Eliann. My body looked more like those of my brothers than it did like hers.

I eased into the water, nearly jumping back out as it froze my flesh. Eliann grinned at me, then sent a second wave up to drown me for a span of shivering breaths. "Come in, Shalene. It will get no warmer standing there." Something shining dropped from her lips and vanished into the pool. It did not swim away so I steeled my courage and plunged into the water after it.

And found myself surfacing in the circle of Eliann's arms. We were nose to nose, and I fell into her silver eyes. Her breasts pressed against mine and the memory of that long-ago day when I kissed her was all I could think about.

I hoped that there wasn't a toad waiting for me.

I wrapped my arms around her and pressed my lips to hers. She tasted of lavender and rich spices, with only a hint of mines and swamp. And I savored all of it, every scent and flavor I could pull from her mouth with my own.

She pressed her lovely naked body against mine and my hands caressed her curves instinctively. After a moment, I became aware that one of her full breasts had floated into my hand and I broke off kissing her mouth to plant feverish kisses on it. Eliann sighed, but the sound soon turned to a deep and fierce groan as my mouth and hands explored all of her that I could reach above and below the water.

Eliann wrapped her legs around my hips and rocked against me as if she were riding a horse. I no longer felt cold; on the contrary, the water warmed as if lit by the sun and I began to give voice to groans of my own. Then she moved her hand between my legs, coaxing new and strange sensations from me, feelings I had never known before. I rode her hand, clasping her fingers inside me until a blinding flash of heat and warmth and lust shook me from head to toe.

"How did you know how to do this?" I gasped at last. "What tutor teaches such things?"

She gave me a slow smile that made me want to see her lose control, to give herself up to me. "The castle library is the safest place to hide if I want to avoid talking to anyone. There are some very instructive"—she broke off with a low, growling moan as I imitated her movements and slipped my fingers inside her before continuing—"texts."

I fumbled against her, trying to use my mouth and my hand and my hips to drive her to the same sensations she had aroused in me. She moved my hand so that my fingers thrust all the way up inside her. I gasped as her cunny walls closed around my fingers and I wondered if I would ever feel my hand again, whole and uncrushed. Then I looked into her lovely half-closed eyes and found that I no longer cared. Instead, I pushed as deep into her as I dared.

She was wet and warm and soft, and our flesh and the water flowed together until I never wanted it to end. This was what I had dreamed of doing, if only I had known it. Why had I let fear and a few toads get in my way?

Eliann gave herself up to me then, her back arching and thrusting her breasts upward to my eager lips. Her legs flailed in the water as I tried to keep her afloat, grateful that the pool was shallow. A series of cries poured from her lips, but not a toad or a gem appeared until she murmured my name, and collapsed, shuddering against me.

Her kisses were hot on my own fevered lips and her hands were everywhere on me until I shivered and shuddered with longings of my own. She bent me over the rocks on the pool's edge and knelt between my thighs, her mouth urgent against the curls where my thighs met. Her fingers were hard, rigid inside me, and I cried out first from the shock of their thrusts, then from pleasure as they coaxed and caressed me, inside and out.

Eliann's tongue drew a circle of fire on my flesh until I howled like one of my father's hounds. With my last bit of will, I dug my fingers into the rocks underneath me to hold myself steady as I bucked and rode her mouth. I surrendered to her touch until I could bear it no longer, and slid off the rocks into the pool, still shivering.

When at last I could speak again, when we had kissed and kissed each other until we drank the air in gulps each time we paused, I looked deep into her silver eyes. "Truly, how did you learn to do such things, Eliann?" I planted a series of little kisses on the bare flesh of her shoulder, trying to warm it with my mouth.

She turned her face aside before she spoke and I realized that she feared to spit out a toad. I vowed then and there that toads would be amongst my favorite creatures if we might know each other like this again. But she spoke before I could tell her so. "I haven't...told you the truth. At least not all of it."

The sound of a discrete cough above our heads made both of us jump. The woman who stood watching us from the bank glowed like the moon and stars. From this alone, I would have known that she was a fairy. But her lovely iridescent wings certainly helped to banish any remaining doubts.

We cringed away from her, such was our surprise and the anger in her coldly beautiful face. I wondered if we had trespassed in her woods, her pool, when I caught a glint of something else, a jealous fury perhaps, in her bright green eyes and her frown. At that moment, her steed shifted forward to drink from the pool and I forgot that thought in my terror.

It raised its great scaled and horned head and uttered a soft growl at us, and Eliann shivered in my arms. But only for a moment before she seemed to draw steel from somewhere deep inside her. She climbed out of the pool and stood on the bank next to our visitor. She had to look up to meet the fairy's eyes, but I saw no terror in her face now. "Hullo, Irista. I wondered when you'd find me." Her tone was curiously calm, resigned, and only a few shining pebbles fell from her lips with her words.

"Well, I certainly didn't expect to find you like this." Irista gestured at me contemptuously and I made a shamefaced effort to cover myself with my hands. Until I realized that Eliann wasn't doing the same and I lowered mine with an effort.

Eliann placed her hands on her shapely and still unclothed hips and said, "Was not your curse enough? Once I was foolish enough to believe that you loved me. I even believed that if I fell in love with you, the curse would be broken. But I did that and nothing changed. Now I believe in neither your lies nor your illusions."

My spirits sank like lead to the bottom of the pool. She loved the fairy who cursed her? Why? She could have anyone, except perhaps Greir or Fenar. She could have me. I would never make her spit up toads.

I watched as Irista trailed a glowing finger down her cheek and Eliann's face seemed to melt. "I had to make sure that you were mine. Only I can break the spell, Eliann. And you know you still love me." Irista's voice came out in a purr and Eliann's shoulders slumped. "Just tell me so and we'll go home. We'll be together always, just as we should be."

She seemed to remember that I was there and glared down at me. "You'll have no need of the likes of her. But then, that's easily fixed now." Her eyes glowed and she gestured to her steed.

Eliann looked startled, her mouth open as if she were frozen in place. I lunged for the bank and my sword as the great beast swung its head around. I rolled forward and grabbed the hilt, just as our old armsmaster had taught. Then I jumped to my feet and confronted the creature, wishing with all my heart that I had time to don my armor.

Irista hissed like a giant snake and urged the beast toward me. That seemed to shake Eliann loose from whatever trance held her. "No! Let her go, Irista. I'll go with you if you let her go!" A white and luminous pearl dropped from her open mouth, and fell to the greensward at her feet.

We all stared at it, with the exception of Irista's beast, which took the opportunity to try and eat me. I slashed it across the snout and danced backward toward the trees. Had Eliann just offered to sacrifice herself for me? Or was it just an excuse to do what she wanted to do anyway? And was this really the best time to worry about that?

The creature slashed out with one great claw, slicing open my leg as I cut into its scales. We both screamed and Eliann screamed with us a breath later when she saw the blood on my leg. Then she was between me and the creature, armed with nothing more than her bare hands. I tried to shove her aside as it lunged, and the giant fangs stopped just short of her head.

I wish that it had been fear of me that stopped its charge but in fact, his mistress's voice filled the clearing with a mighty "Cease!" Irista stalked over to Eliann and I stepped in front of her with my blade up. I stopped it a hairsbreadth shy of her heart and let my face convey my intentions.

She glared down at me, her wings unfurled and her face going dark with rage. I could feel Eliann tremble behind me but instead of trembling myself, I filled with a rage of my own and struck out with my sword. Irista jumped back and held up one glowing hand. Her smile took on an edge that cut through my fury and I braced myself for whatever she was going to do next.

"Irista, no." Eliann's voice was soft, but commanding. I risked a glance over my shoulder and noticed that the ground around her was remarkably toad-free. It was also free of damp flowers and jewels. Her face had a calmness to it that was surprising, given the circumstances. "No," she said again, reaching up first to touch her mouth, then to pull me back to her side. Then she threw her arms wide in a gesture that took in the ground at her feet. "Don't you understand? It was Shalene, Shalene who I really loved all along. Your curse is broken, Irista."

I gaped at her and from the edge of my eye, saw Irista do the same. Eliann looked from the irate fairy to me, then back again. "I'm speaking and there are no toads or jewels or anything else coming out of my mouth. Nothing but words, lovely words!" She started laughing and danced in a little circle. At that moment, Eliann was the most beautiful creature that I'd ever seen and I found myself grinning like a jester.

Irista turned on me with a hissed, "You!" I vowed silently that I would fight her to the death, probably mine, for Eliann's freedom. I prepared to charge.

There followed a loud noise, like a siege engine hitting a wall, and Irista turned a startling shade of green. A shining white object landed at her feet, sending up a pale mist that encircled both her and her mount. Her mouth was moving but I couldn't hear anything she said. This was a welcome relief, given her expression.

After a long moment, she and her creature faded from view, her mouth still open and hands frozen in arcane gestures. I looked at Eliann. "How...how did you know that the pearl would banish her?"

"I didn't. It was just the closest thing I could find to throw to distract her from you. And I thought that since it didn't look like anything that had come out of my mouth before, it might be connected to the curse." Eliann's fingers were gentle on my forgotten wound. "Would you like some company on this quest of yours?" She helped me to sit and placed some wet leaves on my leg. "The one where you win all the valor and the hand of a princess?"

"I think I've found my princess. So perhaps my quest is to discover how to love her and make her happy." I didn't know where the words came from, but I knew they were the right ones. Eliann held me close and we kissed once more, her mouth sweet as dew on mine.

# SWF SEEKS FGM

## Allison Wonderland

*Single Wicked Female Seeks Fairy Godmother for shoe-shopping companion and sappily-ever-after. Must he able to work family-unfriendly magic with wand.*

C hecks have mates. Glass slippers have mates. Even that repulsively scintillating stepdaughter of mine has a mate. Me, I've got bupkis.

As you know, I'm a widow. No, not a black widow—magenta is my color, I'll thank you to remember.

At heart, I'm a simple, vitriolic vixen in search of an animated sorceress who has the power to make my dreams come shrew.

That is to say, true.

I believe what we have here, my dear, is a self-fulfilling prophecy. Once upon a way to pass the time, I married Cinderella's father. We were not even on a first-name basis. I called him My Little Meal Ticket and he called me The Wicked Stepmother, the definite article of which I most definitely found flattering.

In spite of my bad reputation, I made him think my moniker was a misnomer. Damn, I'm good. So when he proposed marriage, I accepted. After all, if I put my mind to it, I could chateau the line.

Everything was copacetic, until my husband croaked like the Frog Prince of a man that he was. Gone were the days of living it up. On the upside, I could once again live up to my nickname.

And did I ever. I looked at that looker Cinderella and thought: *I'll terminate her, too.* Oh, please don't misunderstand me—although my real name is Lady Ptomaine and yes, I did graduate from a Poison Ivy League institution with the highest dishonors, I am by no means a murderess. A villainess, sure, but I can assure you that every one of my husbands departed on good terms.

When Cinderella left—this palace, not this earth—we also parted amicably. I had been so uncouth to the youth, to understate the obvious, yet on her way out of her misery, she opted to hug me instead of slug me. If kindness could kill... Let's just perish the thought, shall we? With all the sincerity I could summon, I wished Cinderella a fond farewell, all the while hoping she would not fare well at all.

But she did, because of course she would. She's the underdog, the heroine. You've all been manipulated into adoring her and abhorring me. It's the age-old tale of good versus evil. When that revoltingly talented songbird brain opens her mouth, it's good verses for her and the evil eye for me.

Why am I so evil? Being mean is a picnic, a cakewalk, as easy as pumpkin pie. When you see, go evil: narrow your eyes like a feline. Mine offers an excellent example. When you hear, go evil: eavesdrop on the conversations of those who are similarly sinister. When you talk, speak pro evil. Use four-letter words such as "hate" and "hurt" and adopt a curt tone when executing commands. You see how straightforward that is?

Speaking of which... Going forward, I am no longer straight. Herein lies the reason for my lies, my manipulations, my machinations. I took to playing cat and mouse with people's feelings as a means of subjugating my own.

I suspect I've always preferred the fair sex over the fair to middling sex—ladies and gentlemen, respectively—but in this kingdom, we are expected to exhibit a proclivity to heteronormativity.

The subject of Sapphic subjects rarely comes up. When it does, when there's any indication, however slight or right, of lady-liking, it's swept under the Magic Carpet, headed off faster than the Queen of Hearts can beseech a beheading.

Remember when Snow White and Princess Aurora, our sleeper hits, hit it off and were caught copulating instead of hibernating?

Or when Ariel, our mouthy mermaid, was discovered muffdiving in Princess Tiana's Black Sea?

Of course you don't. If our underground out newspaper hadn't transcribed these transgressions, I wouldn't either. I recall every word of these human interest stories, which were much more interesting than straight news about Misses becoming Mrs.

Follow-up articles revealed that these princesses were, inevitably, scared straight. It's a small-minded world, after all. I saw that there were two ways of looking at this. I could, as one song advises, blame it on the reign. Or I could take the advice of a more refreshing refrain and believe that gray skies are gonna queer up.

I've put on plenty of things in my day: airs, the blame on others, myself on a pedestal. But a happy face? I wasn't sure that visage was even viable.

Still, I decided to fold up the social ladder and give it a whirl. And do you know what? I triumphed over adversity. Now all I've got to do is triumph over what some might call perversity.

And I just might, mightn't I?

As Fairy Godmothers are inclined to advise, impossible things are happening every gay.

Which brings us to the personal ad I placed in the above-mentioned underground paper. Where I come from, Fairy Godmothers are legendary, lauded for their optimism and altruism and affection for others. A Fairy Godmother, I reasoned, could give me a complete makeover. Internally, of course. Externally, I'm quite fetching, yes? She's mysterious, I'm imperious. She's everything nice, I'm everything vice. We'd make a consummate couple.

That being said, we can't consummate our coupledom until we become a couple. Thus far, I've received a single response to my ad. She telephoned last week, and at first I cringed at the sound of her voice, its treacle tone headache music to my ears. Nevertheless, I provided my address and we agreed to meet today at—

Oh! Queer she is now!

I hustle my bustle to the door and issue greetings and salivations.

That is to say, salutations.

I believe what we have here, my dear, is love at first sight. It is necessary that I describe this magical creature standing before me: in lieu of that joke of a cloak that constitutes the Fairy Godmother uniform, she is outfitted in a black gown that showcases her pleasantly plentiful proportions. Her hair, habitually hidden, is not only visible but luminous and voluminous. I put on a sappy face and glue my gaze to the blue hue of hers.

"You must be Wicked," she says.

"Is that an order," I reply, "or an observation?"

She shakes her head. The expression on her face can only be described as a cross between empathy and enmity.

I offer my arm. She takes it, her grip predictably delicate.

"So you're the devil woman," she remarks, as we embark on our short journey to the sitting room.

"Yes," I gush with pride, "which is why I am in desperate need of a guardian angel."

At this, Godmother scoffs, a response that seems quite out of character for such a winsome woman.

"Why don't you come over here and sit a spell?" I suggest, gesturing to the sumptuous settee that is, at present, bare of bottoms.

Godmother's laugh is polite and a mite patronizing, and her eyes roll over me like the wheels of a horse-drawn carriage. "I see you put the class in classified," she murmurs, settling onto the settee.

A wicked cool heat flickers in my knickers. "It wasn't *that* kind of ad."

Godmother pouts. "I thought that compliment would work to my advantage," she says, and smiles a bashful smile, a dwarf of a thing that makes me...happy?

Is this an emotion I'm even capable of experiencing?

Hmm.

Happiness.

Hmph.

Happiness.

A necessary evil, I suppose. It's a good thing I have someone to help me cope.

Although if I continue to sit here in offensive pensive silence, I'll be on my own. "May I offer you a beverage?"

"No, thank you. I have only a thirst for knowledge." So saying, Godmother leans forward, inspecting the selection of hag rags spread out on the coffee table. She skips over *SinStyle* and *Women's Stealth* and picks up the latest issue of *Good Mousekeeping*.

"That's my baby," I gush, pointing to the handsome, hissyfaced feline on the cover. "He was voted Pussy of the Year by his peers."

"I'd love to meet him," she says, but I can tell she would sooner meet her Maker.

"I'm afraid I can't let him out of the bag. But you know what they say: when the cat's away..." It is then that I notice the magic wand tucked between her breasts. "I envy your bosom friend."

She smirks. "I believe the tail end of that expression is 'the mice will play.'"

For the first time in my life, I hear no evil, only good. "Will they?"

She shrugs. "Will they? Won't they? All perfectly preposterous inquiries that mandate either/or."

"In that case," I snicker, and hope she won't bicker, "are you a man or a mouse?"

"Neither/nor," she answers in all seriousness. "Lady Ptomaine, Bea Strait."

I feel my blood run colder. Is she going to cast aspersions on my perversions? Take that magic wand and poke my eyes out for making eyes at her? "Listen here, you little Fairy Godmotherfu—"

"Don't curse in my presence!" she cries at this sudden absence of innocence.

I feel my ire fire like a flare gun. "How else should I react when you're making insults?"

Godmother is still in the grasp of a gasp. Her expression reminds me of an open casket. Under normal circumstances, that would be a welcome image indeed. However, in spite of my spate of anger, I'd much rather have her in my bed than that in my head.

"I was not making insults," Godmother insists, continuing to shudder in shock. "I was making introductions. Bea isn't a verb.

It's a noun. A proper noun, to be precise. My parents named me after the beauteous Bea Arthur. You should be ashamed of yourself, for goodness's sake."

In response, I hang my head, the way I've seen my inferiors do when I confront or affront them. As my collar chafes my chin, I sense the corners of my mouth turning up instead of down. There's something disturbingly delightful about being disciplined, I discover. As for my venial sin, "God'll get me for that, won't He?"

Bea chuckles. "He'll send you straight to Shady Pines, you shady lady, you." So saying, she reclines against the sofa, properly propping her feet up on the coffee table. Her footwear is fancy: ruby-colored peep-toe shoes that ooze sophistication.

"They're from the Friends of Dorothy Zbornak line," she shares. "Glass slippers really aren't my style. Besides, I could never fill Cinderella's shoes."

Oh, dear. Is she... Could Bea be... "You're *that* Fairy Godmother?" I ask, wringing my hands and sputtering like a lawn sprinkler. Such ignominy. Those of ill repute should never feel ill at ease.

Godmother gives me an all-knowing look. "The one and lonely," she replies.

I should, of course, take my lumps, but I'm afraid I'm a rather amateur apologist. Perhaps I could take them the way I take my coffee: darkly and starkly. Let's give it a whirl, shall we?

"I would like to...express...remorse for behaving like a heel toward Cinderella. It was nothing personal. She and I just got off on the wrong foot, that's all. She really was a shoe-in for the throne. Meanwhile, my girls couldn't even get the shoe on, which should come as no surprise to me because—"

"Listen, lady, put a sock in it, would you? I liked you better when you were unapologetically unapologetic."

Words fail me. I don't know whether to have a good feeling

about this or a bad feeling, although truth be told, I wouldn't know a good feeling if it... I don't know, felt me up.

"You're my type and my stereotype," Bea informs me, surmising my surprise. "If you were expecting me to be the guardian angel to your devil woman, I'm afraid your great expectations are going to grate on my nerves. Oh, that reminds me: Cinderella is expecting."

I blink, experiencing a hint of happy-for-her. It's still an unfamiliar though not entirely irksome emotion. "She's having a baby?"

"No, a ball. Yes, a baby. I'm going to be the baby's godmother—lowercase for the time being, in case somebody else wants the job. I can't hog all the humans, you know. Oh, *that* reminds me—I just love the power of suggestion—before you and I get involved in...an involvement, I've been hearing rumors that you're dating Beauty *and* the Beast."

"I can explain."

"And you will."

I could get used to this, this business of taking orders. As it turns out, it's quite a turn-on. What's more, it's compatible with my motto: it's better to receive than to give.

"Well, you see—"

"Mother!"

"What?" we respond in unison, then chuckle in tandem.

"I have company," I call, in the mother of all motherly tones. "Can it wait?"

"I suppose," one of the girls grumbles. They aren't twins, my daughters, but their unfortunate features render them difficult to look at and, therefore, almost impossible to distinguish. Regardless, I hope they'll accept the Sapphic side of me. They had no choice but to accept the bad side of me, so if need be I'll simply make the choice for them this time too.

Right now, however, I am choosing to focus all my attention

on the very good company sitting beside me. "This rumor, it's unsubstantiated. Ursula started it after I spurned her advances. What could I do? We weren't right for each other. Besides, with as many arms as she's got, she'd never be satisfied with just one octopussy in her garden."

Bea's lips curl like a feline's tail. "So you believe in monogamy?"

"Of course. I may be immoral, but by no means am I amoral."

"Well, it's good to know you haven't lost your touch of evil. I like a dame who's bad news," Bea confesses, and pats my leg just below the thigh. "The Bea's knees," she teases, and squeezes.

So that's what a good feeling feels like. It's not so bad. But I am. Bea said so herself. "You think I'm bad news?" I giggle, the sound more clangorous than languorous, running rings around my daughters' princess phone, although that's not hard, considering it hardly rings.

"Are you quite through?" Godmother inquires, arms tucked under her tits in a way that both complements her pout and demonstrates her clout. "If you're finished, then we can get started."

I can see the oversexed headline in the underground newspaper now: *Bad News Bares All.* My body sizzles like a stake. Er, steak. Naturally, I much prefer the former to the latter. One man's meat is this woman's poison. Hence, no man has ever seen me down at heel.

Alas, no woman has ever brought me to my knees either. "Shall I start at the bottom and work my way down?" I suggest, aiming for that indelicate balance of obscene and obsequious.

"I hear your suggestion and I'll raise you an eyebrow," Godmother replies, and makes good on her word. "I think we ought to keep things G-rated."

I groan, hot under the lavender collar of my dress. "I'd prefer to keep things Bea-rated."

"I think you've been berated enough for one lifetime," Godmother declares, rubbing my back in a spine-tingling show of sympathy. "It's G-rated or nothing. What's it going to be?"

I weigh my options, which are two. Then I weigh my words, which are few: "Is G short for G-spot?"

Bea regards me as though I am one key short of a grand piano. "Well, my evil genius," she replies, her tone transcending condescending and going straight to snooty, "that is spot-on."

My face flushes, and I discover that being red feels far better than seeing red. "I don't mind being put on the spot."

"Then let's get right on it," she enthuses, and uses her hands to hoist me to my feet.

Godmother has more curves than the staircase toward which I'm tugging her, but I must stay ahead of said curves lest she get lost on her first visit to the palace. When we reach the top of the stairs, I make a Bealine for the master bedroom. Master as in mastermind, mind you. I would hate for my boudoir to be mistaken for a male room.

(As you'll note, I am wicked witty when awfully aroused.)

In the privacy of my bedroom, mere seconds after I latch the door, we latch on to each other and share true love's first kiss.

It neither breaks the spell she has over me, nor slakes the dry spell I've been under for the whole of my existence.

Instead, the kiss makes my bliss go from bad to worse, awakening me like the fanfare of a thousand trumpets.

I shoot the messenger a flirty look.

Bea's hand wanders to her wand. She culls it from her cleavage and, with a flourish of the wrist and an infuriatingly infantile incantation, her clothes vanish from her body.

Standing before me, naked as a stripped bed, Bea smirks at my princess-size eyes. "Surely if I can gussy up a girl, I ought to be able to hussy up one too," she reasons, lifting her broad shoulders in a shrug.

"But of course," I murmur, taking in the voluminous view. I marvel at the fluidity of her body. Each curve dips into the next, creating lush, luxurious layers, not unlike the waterfall valance canopy draped to perfection above my bed.

I could just swoon! That is, if I had the faintest idea how.

"Look at you," she coos, "looking longingly at me. So helpless, so harmless, so speechless. My little pine tree, stripped of its bark." Bea tickles the underside of my chin as if I'm a kitten. "Cat got your tongue?"

"Not yet," I purr, as I kneel at the feet of my queen Bea. My lips flex against her sex. "Now it has."

Even this part of her is sickly sweet, but fortunately, this is as good as it wets.

That is to say, gets.

I seize her waist, the supple flesh succumbing to my touch as I plunge my fingers into the smooth grooves of her folds.

My tongue performs matching manipulations, probing every crinkle, provoking every nerve.

I squeeze my way inside and find her cunt rather cozy, like the filling nestled in an éclair.

I can't help but esteem the cream, with its abundant warmth and boundless bounty.

As much as I'd love to linger, however, I think I'd best hit the spot before I put her in a bad one. I'm accustomed to such predicaments, but I sense both desperation and consternation as she raps my head with that hocusy-pocusy rod of hers. Therefore, for once, I would like to do more good than harm.

And so, I thump the bump with my tongue, and remain rooted to the spot, licking with gusto and sucking with spirit.

For her part, Bea jitters and titters, until her composure fritters like a glass slipper.

Bea coming is most becoming.

I rise to my feet and face her.

She looks at me, looks at me licking my lips as I relish the zest of my zaftig.

"Ah, the lady doth ingest too much."

My cheeks burn. Bea holds the royal flush in her hands.

"Let's trade places, shall we?" she suggests, and wields the wand in such a way that I wonder whether she's planning to use it for vanishing purposes or vanquishing ones.

She moves impossibly queer.

That is to say, near.

I want her so bad—the only way I can want her, of course.

"Whoever thought," Bea muses, as she grips then rips my dress, "that *I'd* be known as an evildoer?"

# THE MARK
# AND THE CAUL

## Annabeth Leong

A desperately poor woman gave birth to a baby girl and rejoiced because the child came into the world with her face hidden by a caul. The woman knew that sailors would pay good coin for the bit of flesh, since legend told that it would protect its bearer from drowning.

As soon as she recovered from her time abed, the woman walked with the baby and the caul to the riverside docks to find a sailor. In a loud and dirty inn, she negotiated a transaction that would keep her family fed for several weeks and even allow them to buy a little meat. She turned toward the door with a smile, but before she could escape, an ancient soothsayer grabbed her by the elbow.

"Let me tell the child's future," creaked the crone.

The woman would have dodged away, but the sailor raised his glass and demanded a prophecy, and she did not wish for him to change his mind about the coin he'd given her.

The soothsayer brushed her thumb through the soft, black hair atop the baby girl's head, and peered into her still unfocused eyes. "I see a life of good fortune," she intoned. The onlookers at the bar drank to that and cheered, and the poor woman tried again to tug free. The soothsayer's grip remained strong. "At nineteen," she continued, "the babe will marry the king's daughter."

The bar's patrons burst into guffaws, for they knew the child was a girl. The soothsayer frowned, and the poor woman hugged her daughter closer. One never wished to anger those with strange powers—a prediction of good fortune could become a curse at any moment. She bowed deeply. "Thank you, Mother. I will hold your words close to my heart." The moment she could, she broke away and returned home, praising God for her windfall.

The poor woman thought no more of the soothsayer's prophesy, but the sailor carried the story far and wide, laughingly repeating it to any who would listen. Before long, it reached the ear of King Harold himself. Rather than waving the prophecy away with a chuckle, as his advisors did, the king, who was a deeply superstitious man, spent several sleepless nights pondering its meaning.

He intended for his daughter, Lucinda, to marry a neighboring king as soon as she was of age. Over barley wine, he and his friend had hammered out the details of the marriage before Lucinda was born, and the king was looking forward to the strategic trade routes he would control as a result of the union. What's more, King Harold was disturbed by the thought of his daughter bound in an unnatural union with another woman.

He made his decision and set out to find the baby girl who had been born with a caul. Thanks to the king's money and power, the task was not difficult, and before long, he disguised himself as a wealthy foreign merchant and knocked at the poor woman's door.

"Good woman," the king said, "will you give your daughter

to me to raise as my own? While conducting business in the capital, I met a sailor who told me that your babe was born to a prophecy of good fortune, and I have always wished for a child."

The woman was skeptical, but the king displayed a great sum of money and suggested that being adopted by a sought-after businessman was a perfect example of the sort of luck that would feature in the girl's life.

At last, he convinced the baby's mother. He paid her handsomely and rode with the child a long distance down the river, where he placed the baby in a box and threw her into deep water. Satisfied that he had disposed of this most unwanted "suitor," he returned to his palace.

The king, however, had forgotten that a babe born in a caul cannot drown. Instead of sinking, the box sailed down the river all the way to the capital, where it came to rest on the bank beside a mill.

The miller's wife, now past childbearing age, had long lamented her infertility. Walking by the river that evening, she heard a cry and was overjoyed to discover the baby girl. She took the child to her husband, and they agreed to raise her and teach her all they knew. They named her Sam, and she grew up strong and lovely, kind and clever with a needle but also bold and handy with the mill's machines. In thanksgiving for this unexpected blessing, they left a meal for the river's spirit in the sand at the water's edge on each new moon, and they carried this out faithfully for nineteen years.

One day, King Harold set out on a journey and got caught in a thunderstorm at the outskirts of the capital. His party had recently passed near the mill, and he returned to that place and asked for shelter. Noticing the strapping youth who took his men's horses, the king asked the miller if his son would grumble about having to work in the driving rain.

"No," the good man replied. "Wet doesn't bother that one—never did. Sam—strong as a boy but our daughter nonetheless—came to us nineteen years ago, sailing along the river in a box without a care in the world."

The king understood what must have happened, and he turned away and ground his teeth. Composing himself, he pasted on a pleasant expression and asked the miller for a favor. "I wish to send a letter to the queen. Since your Sam won't mind the rain, could she carry it to my wife? I'll give two gold pieces for the trouble."

The miller readily agreed, and the king penned a note to his Queen Matilda: "I expect to find the bearer of this letter dead and buried when I come back."

Sam tucked the letter inside her cloak and set out into the storm, whistling. She ordinarily possessed an excellent sense of direction, but on this occasion she missed a signpost and became lost in the large forest that separated the palace from the capital city. After wandering well into the night, Sam noticed a glimmering light in the distance and walked toward it.

The light led to a small house hidden behind a stand of nine hazel trees. The rain crackled into a round pool beside the house, where bright fish swam to and fro. Sam approached without fear and knocked at the door to the house. There were rustling sounds from within, and after several long minutes, the door was flung open. Sam stood before a plump figure covered from head to toe in black cloth. "What business have you here?"

The query took Sam aback, for it had been spoken not in the crone's voice she anticipated but in the soft, sweet tones of a maid. She did not let her surprise show, however. "I have come from the mill," Sam replied. "I am carrying a letter to the queen, but I've lost my way. Would it disturb you very much to allow me to stay here for the remainder of the night?"

The hidden woman peered at Sam. Her head cloth slipped to one side, and Sam glimpsed peculiar pale markings on the dark cheeks beneath it. "There is only one bed," she stammered.

"That does not trouble me," said Sam.

"Robbers sleep here sometimes."

Sam raised an eyebrow. "Do they?"

"They could."

"If the favor is a bother to you, madam, I'll find another place to lay my head." She quirked up a corner of her mouth. "It's a little damp out, is all."

Sam turned away, but before she could disappear from the circle of light, the woman in the house called her back. "Wait!"

"Yes?"

"A favor for a favor?"

"Of course."

Now, the figure who greeted Sam was actually Lucinda. She had discovered the small house in the woods as a young girl, when it had belonged to an old wise woman. Charmed by the hedge witch's bubbling pots and fragrant herbs, she had seized any chance to retreat there. The old woman had extracted an odd promise from the princess—if she ever disappeared, Lucinda was to catch and eat a fish from the pool beside the house. Lucinda, however, had been approaching the cottage one day unnoticed by her mentor, and had seen the old woman jump into the pool. When she failed to come up for air, Lucinda had run to the pool but found only fish swimming there. The old woman never returned, but Lucinda had ever after feared the nature of the fish, and had not been able to bring herself to fulfill her promise. Instead, she snuck to the small house whenever she could, and did her best to keep it tidy and ready for the wise woman's return.

The arrival of the stranger from the mill presented a unique opportunity to discover what had become of the hedge witch. "I need you to dive into the pool beside the house," Lucinda said, "and bring me whatever you find at the bottom."

"Now?" Sam asked incredulously. "In the dark? In the storm?"

Lucinda had rarely been denied anything, and she ducked her head in shame. She wondered how often her commands would have been met with this response had she not been born to luxury. "I suppose the request is foolish. I apologize."

Sam's jaw worked as she stared back at Lucinda. After a moment, she shrugged. She swam well and trusted the water. "No more foolish than anything else." She walked to the pool, shedding her clothes as she went.

Lucinda could not take her eyes off this strange woman. Sam wore the clothes of a man, but the body that emerged beneath them, all compact muscle and firm curves, was undeniably feminine. Sam took down her hair from its leather thong, then twisted it into a tighter knot and retied it. She tossed a look over her shoulder at Lucinda and plunged into the pool.

Lucinda's mouth went dry. She had heard her handmaids tittering about the charms of noble youths, but no young man had ever incited the stirrings in her body that Sam did. While Lucinda appreciated the aesthetics of Sam's powerful body, she truly could not resist the knowing twinkle that had been in her eye, as if she saw straight through Lucinda's black garments, and even through her persona as princess. It was the first look that had made Lucinda feel like a woman.

Her hands shook, but there was another reason to have sent Sam to the bottom of the pool, and she knew she could not squander the opportunity. Searching quickly through Sam's clothing, Lucinda found the letter addressed to her mother. She unfolded it and saw her father's seal and the command inside, and her guts twisted so painfully that she nearly forgot to conceal what she had done before Sam returned to the surface.

Dripping water, Sam drew in deep breaths. She showed her upturned palm to Lucinda. "I found precious little down there," she said. "Only some hazelnuts."

Lucinda frowned. "That is puzzling." It would not have pleased her if Sam had found the wise woman's body, but it would have settled the mystery of her disappearance.

"Are you searching for something in particular? You need only ask, and I will dive to the bottom of the pool again."

"I have only the one favor to offer in return."

"I hardly believe that," Sam replied. "But I require no payment. I would do the deed simply for the asking."

Lucinda stiffened. Sam made her feel naked even while clothed. Her body heated under the wise woman's black garments and she knew that, given the chance, she would offer all her most tender favors to Sam. She wished she could fling herself at the other woman and take her in her arms, but she lacked the courage to lay herself bare as Sam had done.

She collected her thoughts. "You are kind, but there is no need for you to dive again. I trust that you searched well the first time. Come. Let us eat the hazelnuts together."

Sam nodded and gathered up her clothes. Lucinda swallowed her disappointment as the other woman covered herself again. Returning to the house, she put the hazelnuts over the fire to roast and mixed a few of the wise woman's dried herbs to make tea.

As she worked, she questioned Sam about what she knew of the king, but could discover no reason for his animosity. She could not bear to see glorious Sam cut down in her prime, and so she devised a plan.

Lucinda dropped a pinch of a powerful sleeping herb into Sam's tea, then sat beside the fire and ate hazelnuts with her until the other woman began to nod off. Before she succumbed completely, Lucinda helped her to the bed. Sam fell fast asleep the moment her head hit the pillow. For a while, Lucinda stood still and stared, trying to define what about this woman's face affected her so. She found no answer, only a continued desire to look.

Removing her father's letter from the sleeping Sam's cloak, Lucinda took it to the wise woman's writing desk. She carefully imitated her father's handwriting and transferred his seal to create a new message. "The moment the bearer of this letter arrives, she is to be married to our daughter. Waste no time ordering the feast and arranging the great event."

Lucinda tore up the original and burned the pieces. She tucked the forgery into Sam's cloak, took one more longing glance, put out the fire, and returned to the palace to make herself ready.

Sam awoke to find the ashes of the fire cold and scattered, and her mind groggy. No sign remained of the woman she had met the night before, but the memory of her dark eyes made Sam's heart quiver in her chest. In the light of day, she could see many strange and magical objects decorating the inside of the house, and she feared that the woman had ensorcelled her. She shut up the house with care, and continued carrying out the king's errand. Sam was quite relieved to discover a road she recognized, and she did her best to forget the strange encounter.

She arrived at the palace and, after displaying the king's seal on the letter she carried, was brought before Queen Matilda. The queen read the letter, and then stared at Sam for several long moments. "What do you know of my daughter?" she asked finally.

"Only that she is said to be very beautiful," Sam replied.

The queen understood from this that Sam knew nothing of Lucinda, for the princess had been born with a large white birthmark covering the lower half of her face, and no one had ever called her beautiful. She folded the letter and considered.

"Did my husband speak to you before giving you this letter?"

"Only to command that I bring it to you."

She could not guess why the king would order her to perform this unusual wedding, but for her own reasons the idea appealed to her. Queen Matilda had long disliked the neighboring king to whom Lucinda was promised. When she had realized her daughter would never be beautiful, the queen had become afraid that this man would mistreat or demean her. The common woman before her might indeed make a more suitable spouse for Lucinda, the queen thought, but she had to be sure.

"What is the value of a woman?" asked the queen. "Does it lie in her beauty?"

"Beauty seems like a valuable thing," Sam said. "It affects the way a person is seen and spoken to. But I think the real value of a woman lies in the quality of her soul, and that this would be the same for any person. After all, we are taught that the spirits beyond fight over the fate of all our souls, not only those of the beautiful."

"What of wealth? Should a person marry for it?"

"Wealth is pleasant to have. Few would be disappointed to gain it, and some must marry or have nothing at all. For my part, I wish most of all for my husband to treat me kindly and with respect, as I have seen my father do for my mother. I would marry a poorer man if it meant receiving this."

"And must a woman marry a man? What if you were to marry a woman instead?"

Sam could not understand the reason for these questions, but she did not want to hesitate before the queen. She answered as honestly as she could. "I have never considered the idea, but I see no reason not to."

"Do you think you could love a woman?"

Sam thought back to the previous night and the strange way the black-clad woman had made her feel. "I believe I could."

"Wait here."

The queen disappeared into the depths of the palace, and Sam stood uncomfortably among the guards, wondering why she had not been dismissed. Soon, she noticed increased foot traffic in the hallway outside the room where she had been received. More time passed, and the palace began to bustle.

A guard appeared, dressed in the queen's livery, and commanded Sam to follow him. Sam swallowed her fear and asked for an explanation, but the man refused to give one. He took Sam to lavish chambers where she spent the remainder of the day being groomed in ways she had never previously imagined possible. At last, she was dressed in finery from head to toe. The guard returned, took her by the arm, and led her to the palace chapel.

Sam caught sight of her bewildered adoptive parents in seats of honor, thought back to the queen's questions, and realized that she was about to wed Lucinda. As guards guided her into position, she searched her heart for her honest reaction. It was certainly an honor to wed a princess, but Sam worried that she would not know how to be a spouse to Lucinda. And what if the princess had an unpleasant disposition? What if she was unhappy about being wed to Sam? Another thought of the black-clad woman flickered through her head, and a part of her lamented never being able to visit the small house beside the pool again.

Then court musicians began to play flutes and timbrels, and Lucinda appeared at the other end of the chapel. A white veil covered the lower half of her face, but Sam would have known those eyes anywhere. If this was witchcraft, she didn't mind. Her body relaxed, and she carried out the ceremony with cautious anticipation.

Sam was in a daze by the time the wedding concluded and the celebration began. Courtiers offered the newlywed couple gifts of grains, dried fruit, and sweets. Lucinda was dressed in a cloak made of pearls and helped into a litter, which was carried by six stout men. The men held her aloft and displayed her for hours, until their strength gave out. When they put her down at last, Lucinda stepped into Sam's arms for the first time.

To Sam, everything in the world disappeared at that moment except for her new wife. Lucinda's thick, curly hair still smelled of roasted hazelnuts, and her lush curves fit and mingled with Sam's muscular form.

When the princess pulled back, Sam saw they had been left alone. She bent to Lucinda's ear. "Why am I married to you? Surely there is no shortage of princes—or princesses—who would be overjoyed to be in my position, and I am only a commoner."

Lucinda raised one thick eyebrow, and a serious expression flashed through her dark eyes. "You've married me because that was my wish. But there is much we must discuss in private."

"Who are you really?"

"I'm the woman who was born when you climbed out of the pool and looked at me."

Lucinda led Sam to her private chambers. As they navigated the hallways, Sam planned the questions she would ask once they got there, but when they arrived, Lucinda shut the door and turned to face her, and all words fell away.

Sam traced the curve of Lucinda's ear, ending at one edge of the concealing veil. "May I?"

"Perhaps you had better not." Tears glistened in her eyes.

"Why?"

"The way you look at me will change. Please. Give me just one day like this. I want to see you desiring me. That playful smirk of yours. I can't bear for it to disappear just yet."

Sam felt her lips flatten into a serious line. She wondered what horrors lay under the veil but was careful not to reveal any worry or disgust. She thought for a moment, and then realized what she needed to say to her new wife. "I fell for your eyes, which I have seen and am seeing now. If that's all you will show me, then I understand, and it is enough. More than enough. A blessing." Sam dropped her hands to her sides, away from Lucinda, and waited.

Lucinda cupped Sam's cheek. "You see? This is why I've married you. I can imagine no other spouse who would say such a thing to me, and truly mean it. Is it unfair if I ask you to let me see you again? You seemed unafraid last night, and I thought perhaps you would be willing now."

Sam hesitated, and Lucinda drew back, covering her face with one hand. "I am making too many requests," Lucinda said. "I have done nothing but ask you for favors since the moment we met."

At this, Sam's smile returned. She tugged gently at Lucinda's hand so she could look into her eyes again. "If I remember correctly, it was I who began our acquaintance with a request for a favor. And now, despite your wisdom, you've not got the right of it. It is a favor to me for you to look at me. It is a favor for you to let me reveal myself to you."

Sam made good on her words, undoing her clothing for Lucinda. She handled the fine fabrics lightly and with care, and as she undid hooks from eyes, she made sure to look upon Lucinda with heat in her gaze, silently promising to exercise this deftness on her new wife in the future. She shrugged herself clear of the costly garments, and to Lucinda, Sam's body seemed even finer naked and unadorned.

"May I touch you?" Lucinda asked.

"You may do with me as you please."

Lucinda stepped close. At first, despite her question, she touched only with eyes, her fingers too timid to bridge the gap between them. When she lifted a hand at last, she flitted it around Sam's body like a butterfly too skittish to alight. Feeling ridiculous, she brought a fingertip to rest on the blunt tip of Sam's broad nose.

They both froze, and then Sam laughed, and the sound freed Lucinda to gather her wife into her arms more boldly. She learned the shapes of Sam's shoulder blades, the curve of her spine, and the solidity of her hips. She tucked Sam's muscular buttocks into the palms of her hands, but the powerful response in her body alarmed her and she retreated to Sam's elbows. Lucinda, however, could not resist stroking upward from there, outlining her wife's upper arms, which were strong and thick from helping the miller.

This supposedly less intimate territory still made Lucinda's stomach flutter. She rested the side of her face between Sam's breasts, barely trusting her legs to hold her up. Wrapping one arm around Sam's back, Lucinda allowed her other hand to wander to the hollow of Sam's throat, over the point of one taut breast, along the side of her rib cage, and finally, between her legs.

"Moon above and river below," Sam cursed.

Lucinda smiled at the reaction and petted the damp hair that grew over Sam's pubis. She knew the pleasure her own body yielded when she explored this place. "There is a river below indeed. I feel the signs of its presence, though I have not found it yet."

Sam widened her stance. "You seem clever enough to track it."

"You will not be able to remain standing under the force of its waters once I make them flow," Lucinda said. She led her wife to her bed and helped her in. Then she rubbed the top of one of Sam's thighs, as if she were a great mill horse in need of steadying. Slowly, Lucinda parted her wife's lower lips, revealing the extent of her wetness.

"Ah," Sam sighed. "You've found it."

"I've found the path that leads there." Lucinda began a thorough examination of the territory, at first simply stroking and discovering, then later responding to the hiss of Sam's breath and the catches in her throat. She trapped sensitive flesh between her first two fingers, squeezing lightly, tugging, and rolling.

Sam gave a full-throated cry, and her firm body became rigid and hard beneath Lucinda's touch. Pleasure shattered off her and pounded through the room, rolling from Sam's body in waves that Lucinda could feel at her temples. Sam gasped, and finally caught her breath. "My mother told me the pleasures of the marriage bed were not for women," she said at last. "I've never known her to be wrong before, and yet I can imagine nothing sweeter than what you have done to me."

Lucinda stretched out beside Sam, still in her clothes. She slipped her hand beneath her veil so she could inhale Sam's scent, and shivered all over at the spice of it. "It heartens me to hear this from you. I was always told that it would hurt."

Sam clutched Lucinda fiercely. "I swear I'll never hurt you."

"I know you won't."

"Will you let me please you, too?"

Lucinda drew a deep breath. "Soon," she promised. "But not yet."

Sam nodded and held her, and the two women whispered secrets to each other.

On the first few mornings after that, Lucinda started their day by asking if she could keep her veil. Sam always agreed. On the fifth morning, Sam stopped her before she could speak. "It's your veil," she said. "You don't need my permission to wear it." The agreement made, they lived together in bliss for several weeks, Lucinda caressing Sam everywhere by night and Sam righting insecurities with a lopsided smile. They fell more deeply in love each day, but they knew that trouble would return along with Lucinda's father, the king.

"Tell him you carried the message faithfully, and you never saw any sign that it had been changed," Lucinda implored Sam.

Sam scowled and paced the room. "You would have me risk being trapped by my own words."

They debated and discussed endlessly, and when the trumpets signaled that King Harold had indeed arrived, they had planned no concrete strategy for facing his wrath.

When King Harold entered the palace and learned what had happened, he called Queen Matilda to him at once. He roared and raged, flinging candlesticks and tearing tapestries down from the walls. The queen handed him the letter that Sam had delivered and refused any further conversation while he exhibited such wildness. The king examined the letter and saw that, though the writing closely resembled his, it had not come from his hand. He called Sam to a private audience.

She arrived humbly, dressed in the minimum of finery appropriate to her new station, and knelt before the king.

"You are a clever forger," the king said in a low, dangerous voice. "Your artifice has won you the bride you've always wanted, the one you were destined for."

Sam glanced up in surprise. "Your Majesty, I don't understand you. I have grown to love your daughter a great deal in a short time, but trust and believe that I never dreamed of desiring such a bride until I found myself dressed in wedding clothes."

The king, too angry for discretion, told Sam the story of her birth. Sam's face grew pale as she learned how she had been tricked away from her mother and nearly drowned. A muscle in the side of her neck twitched, and she clenched her teeth.

When the king had finished speaking, Sam rose deliberately to her feet. "I suppose you can have me killed for this," she said, "but I won't kneel to a man who twice tried to murder me through devious means. If I am to die by your hand, I will have it happen honestly. I would never have so much as breathed

Lucinda's name until you sent me here, but now that we are wed, I will love her to my dying breath."

King Harold signaled a guard to cut Sam down, but at that moment, Lucinda, who had been listening from just outside the chamber, ran in and flung her arms around her wife. "You must run through me as well, Father. I cannot lose her."

The guard hesitated, and the king stared. He thought of his old friend in the neighboring kingdom and that long-ago night with the barley wine. They had grown apart since then, neither the trade routes nor the daughter as attractive as they had once expected. He thought of the way Lucinda would certainly howl with prolonged grief if he did this thing. It occurred to him that this was a petty reason to spare a person's life, but he had taken and spared lives for far less.

He glared at his daughter and her veiled, ugly face, and realized who the real forger must be. King Harold knitted his eyebrows into a stern expression. "I believe this is a forgery of a marriage, but I will give you a chance to prove that it is not. Your marriage must, of course, have issue. If you are fruitful, then I will accept you both—I will even make Sam here the crown, uh, princess. If a year passes with no sign that Lucinda is with child, however, then I must make room for a man who can give Lucinda an heir." He gave a horrible smile. "You take my meaning, of course."

Sam squared her shoulders. "Perfectly." Solutions already filled her mind. She would not risk their happiness over jealousy, and Sam was certain that a tolerable man could be found to stand in for husbandly duties. She squeezed Lucinda's hand to reassure her, and led her toward the door.

King Harold stopped them before they could escape. "Keep in mind," he purred, "that if any man can claim the child as his own, I'll have to punish my daughter for adultery."

When they returned to Lucinda's chamber, their mood was

hopeless. Sam clasped Lucinda around the waist. "We'll have a year together. Many people lack even that much love."

"If only I could think of something to try," Lucinda said, but then fell silent. In her excitement over her marriage, she had forgotten the small house beside the pool, and the old woman's last request.

She told Sam the story, and called her favorite guard to the chamber. A heavy coin purse secured his assistance helping them slip out of the palace unnoticed, as it had for her many times before. "Be back before sunrise," he whispered as they left.

The rain began again as Sam and Lucinda made their way through the woods. When they arrived at the stand of hazel trees, Sam pulled off her clothes and dove into the pool. At once, a salmon swam into her arms, bright, iridescent, and heavy. Her powerful thighs strained to lift it out of the pool.

Lucinda waited at the shore. With grim efficiency, she gutted and cleaned the fish while Sam built a fire.

Placing the fish in a heavy metal pan, she and Sam watched in silence as it sizzled.

The fish's fat hung heavy in the air in the small house. "I am here for you whatever happens," Sam said.

Lucinda took a small helping and lifted one bite to her lips. When she swallowed it, she cried out. Sam sprang to her side. "What is it? What can I do?"

Lucinda turned to her wife, her eyes wide. "I saw a star being born in the night sky, so white and yet so hot. I saw its light traveling for thousands of years, and I know when it will reach us here."

Sam frowned. "Do you feel well?"

"So far." Lucinda took another bite. Each one brought a startling new revelation. She saw thick snakes that swam in rivers on the other side of the world. She saw the paths tracked by currents through the ocean. She saw the rivers of fire that flow beneath the surface of the earth. She took another helping and saw how people lived before kings and how they would live after them.

"You should eat this with me," Lucinda said. "The wise woman gave me everything she knows, and I can share it with you."

Sam patted Lucinda's knee. "I don't think I could hold all that. She entrusted this to you for good reason. If there's anything I really ought to know, you can tell me about it the old-fashioned way."

Lucinda ate until her mind was full, but much of the fish still remained. She knew she could not waste it, and so she continued eating. Since the knowledge had nowhere else to go, it spilled into her womb. Her belly began to swell.

She gripped Sam's fingers tightly as she continued eating, whispering to her about the child she could see, a girl as wise as her mentor but as bold and lucky as Sam. Realizations lit Lucinda's mind in bursts like fireflies on a still summer night.

She had seen the wisdom of the ages, and yet, as she took her last bite, one last small thing washed through her with greater force than the explosion at the dawn of the universe. She snapped her dark eyes open, and Sam gasped, for they twinkled with multitudes of stars.

Holding Sam's gaze, Lucinda fumbled with her veil and tore it free. "I'm not ugly," she said, her voice heavy with wonder.

The white birthmark that Lucinda had covered all her life was, to Sam, a thrilling unknown, a reflection of the caul that had heralded Sam's own journey into the world. She wondered if it, too, gave luck, and which woman's luck had brought them together. Sam touched the princess's cheeks with both hands, kissed her lips, and stroked her chin and jaw. "You're so beautiful."

Lucinda stood and snatched away her ever-present coverings, unveiling herself fully. It felt as if she were being born, and she marveled at how often Sam's presence could renew her.

"Touch me," Lucinda whispered.

Sam put both hands on her bare, swelling belly, and they both felt the spark of life within. "Your father will have to accept this," Sam said. "You're with child, and no man can claim it as his own."

Lucinda smiled. She trembled from all that she had taken in, and more than anything she needed Sam's touch to release some of that pressure. She guided her wife's hands to cup her heavy breasts. "It's yours, too," Lucinda said. "I would never have had the courage if not for you. And I'm yours."

Sam drew her close, kissing the outline of the birthmark, teasing her nipples awake and pressing fingers between her legs until Lucinda threw her head back and glimpsed a different world altogether.

# PENTHOUSE 31

## Brey Willows

B ren Ryder ran her forearm over her face to keep the sweat from dripping into her eyes. The salt in her new Celtic tattoo stung like a bitch, but she ignored it. When you were thirty stories up, suspended by ropes and pulleys, it was a damn bad idea to get distracted. The late afternoon sun glinted off the tower windows in front of her, making her glad she'd remembered her sunglasses before rushing out into the foggy San Francisco morning.

The high-rise she was working on required constant maintenance, and as she checked the seals around the windows, she usually did her best to avoid actually looking inside. Too many times to count she'd glanced in to see some couple getting it on, or someone doing drugs. Once she'd seen someone lying on the floor, obviously not in a good state based on the amount of blood around them, and she'd called the police from twenty stories up. But it always amazed her when women walked through the place naked, even though she was clearly on the other side of the glass. Plenty had given her a little show, something she never minded, although it left her uncomfortably aroused for the rest of the day, her boxers wet and irritating.

The one set of windows, however, that she always looked forward to checking, was the penthouse at 31. It was massive, and the windows went nearly all the way around. Even the bedroom was floor-to-ceiling windows, but that had black-out blinds. She had caught glimpses of the beautiful woman who lived there, seemingly alone, several times. She was usually curled up on the couch, her exceptionally long brown hair pulled into a ponytail, glasses perched on the end of her cute little nose, her feet tucked under her, and a laptop balanced on her lap. Without fail, whenever Bren was working on her windows, the woman stopped whatever she was doing and watched Bren the way a child watches animals at the zoo. Bren stole glances, sucked in her stomach, flexed her arms. There was something sensual about the woman, something intense but vulnerable. Bren desperately wanted to get to know her, but professionally she couldn't possibly ask the woman's name or number. Hell, she'd have to shout through the glass to find out, and that just seemed stupid.

But whenever she knew she'd be checking 31, she wore her shirt with the cut-off sleeves that showed off her biceps, and the jeans that were just a bit tighter. With all the straps and wires, and the heavy tool belt she wore, the jeans were practically invisible, but it made her feel sexier anyway. She loved when the woman watched her, and for some reason it really, intensely mattered that the woman liked what she saw.

Today the living room was empty. Bren allowed herself a moment to look, really look, at the interior. Although the windows had privacy coating, up this close it was easy to see inside. A massive canvas sat on an enormous easel. Bren squinted to get a better look. It appeared to be a castle. Not a childish one, but one out of some kind of dark fantasy. Shrouded in fog, surrounded by threatening trees under an ominous sky. A figure stood in a window, her long hair caught by an invisible breeze as it hung from the high terrace. The overall scene was so lonely, so intense and sad, that Bren wondered what went through the woman's mind as she was painting it. Did she feel as isolated as the woman in the painting?

A movement in the corner of her eye startled her and she jumped slightly, sending her ropes and cords swaying enough to make her nervous. The woman stood in the doorway to the bedroom, watching her. As always it was a look of avid curiosity, like a cat searching for movement in tall grass, rather than irritation at having caught Bren blatantly staring inside her home.

Bren gave her a brief smile and quickly returned to work, checking the seals and bolts the way she was supposed to. When she got to the dining room window, her stomach dropped. A hairline crack ran along one edge, radiating from a circular divot. *Probably caused by a bird hit.* It wasn't serious, but it could be. Glass shattering and falling from this high up would certainly kill anyone below it, and if the person inside was standing too close, it could do them some damage too. The thought of the mystery woman getting hurt in any way made her feel a bit ill.

She made a note of the exact length and location of the crack before she moved on, checking the rest of the windows carefully. If the bird had been with a flock, there could have been other hits, but by the time she'd made her way almost all the way around, she was relieved to find the rest of the windows secure. She had just finished inspecting the last window, almost opposite where she started, when she saw the front door open.

It was the first time she'd seen anyone else enter the apartment, and she couldn't help but stop to see who the woman's visitor was. The window she was hanging outside of was far enough to the side that the person coming in wouldn't see her right away, and she felt distinctly shady peering inside. If she had needed to guess what type of visitor the woman would have, it wouldn't have been the stately, scary-looking older woman who walked in. She didn't so much walk as glide, and her jet-black hair, peppered with gray, was offset by the black leather coat draped over her shoulders. Her face was long and gaunt, her eyes hollow. Bren felt herself shrink away involuntarily.

The beautiful woman appeared in the doorway of the bedroom and seemed to brace herself against it. Bren knew body language, and the younger woman's body was screaming her discomfort. She watched as the older woman gestured disdainfully at the younger woman before making herself a drink. She stood in front of the painting, studying it as she sipped her drink. The young woman never moved from her place in the doorway, but Bren saw her glance through the window at her before returning her attention to the woman. That one glance held more sadness and desperation than Bren had ever seen in a person's eyes. It made her heart ache, and her curiosity about the situation in Penthouse 31 intensified.

She began her descent, slowly releasing the pulley system that kept her suspended. Something about the older woman made her think it would be bad to be caught peeping into the apartment, even though part of her hated the thought of leaving the young woman there, as idiotic as that was. It was slow going, and although her mind was whirling with what she'd seen, she made sure to keep her attention on what she was doing, since plummeting to her death wasn't going to help her situation at all. When she made it to the bottom her arms ached from the strain and sweat soaked her shirt.

Joe, another inspector, sat on the hood and held out a cold soda. "All right?"

She took a long swig of the drink. "Yeah. Crack in Penthouse 31, probably a bird strike. Far left."

He whistled and looked up. "That would be a damn lot of glass."

She nodded. "I'll call it in."

"Sad, though. You'll probably have to do the fix from the outside. Won't be let in."

She turned back to him quickly. "What do you mean? Why?"

He nodded toward the penthouse. "Jamie O'Cairn. She's got that disease, you know, the one where people are afraid to go outside? My wife is a big fan of her paintings, all dark and scary. I won't let her hang any in the bedroom, too freaky for me. Rumor is she's been that way for a lot of her life." He took a drink and continued to look up, looking pensive. "Imagine, shutting yourself away in a tower like that." He laughed. "Like some princess in a fairy tale."

Bren grinned, but she couldn't shake the feeling of unease. Somehow the fact that the beautiful woman was stuck up there, with that horrible woman visiting her, did seem absurdly fairy tale like. She shivered at the memory of the look in the woman's eyes. She grabbed the phone to distract herself.

"Hey boss. Yeah, mostly good. Crack in Penthouse 31, probably a bird strike. Single, far left, seven millimetres. What do you want to do?"

She listened as her boss typed whatever info it was he processed into his computer. "It's Friday, and I don't want to leave something like that any longer than necessary. Was there anyone home?"

"Yeah. A woman. Joe says she's some kind of shut-in, though."

"Well, shut-in shouldn't be an issue. You're not asking her to leave. See if she'll let you inspect the window from the inside. If the crack goes all the way through, we'll get someone out first thing in the morning for a reinstall. If not, we'll do it Monday. Either way, let her know."

Bren closed her eyes. *This is it.* Her chance to meet the woman who often slid through her dreams like smoky silk, her chance to see that pretty face up close. "Cool. I'll let you know what she says."

She went back to the truck and started removing the various harnesses that surrounded her. She was inordinately glad she'd worn her best work shirt and jeans. Granted, she was sweaty and dirty, and probably looked like hell, but hey, it was better than being completely scruffy.

She entered the main lobby, and realized she looked far scruffier than she hoped. Compared to the marble reception area, the slate-black tiled floor, the white countertops, she looked like someone had just poured a bit of earth into a museum.

"Can I help you?" The receptionist looked like she was trying not to wrinkle her nose in distaste.

"I'm with the window inspection crew. I need to talk to the resident in the penthouse on 31 about a potential problem."

The girl bit her lip, suddenly seeming far less confident. "I don't...I mean...she can't be bothered."

Bren sighed. "Look, I won't bother her. But the crack could be dangerous, and you don't want her hurt, do you? Or someone on the street below if that window falls out?"

The girl paled. "Well, no, of course not. Let me call."

Bren noticed that her hand shook slightly and frowned. *What the hell?* It didn't seem like normal concern for a resident. She seemed...scared.

"Yes, Ms. O'Cairn? The window inspector, she's found a problem. She needs to see your window." She waited a moment, then seemed to relax slightly. "Yes, I'm sorry, I didn't see her leave. Thank you, I'll send the inspector up." She hung up and turned back to Bren, looking slightly calmer. "I'll key you up to her floor."

She walked ahead of Bren, who couldn't help but notice the

small, firm ass under the tight, short skirt. She looked away quickly when the girl pressed her card to the elevator, then swiped it quickly inside before pressing the level for the penthouse. The elevator opened into a small entryway, and she raised her hand to knock, but the door opened before she could.

And there she was. Her beautiful long hair was held up in a complicated braid like a crown, but was still long enough to hang down her back to her heels. Her eyes were brown, like milk chocolate flecked with bits of dark chocolate. Her lips were on the thin side, pastel pink. And they were turned up in the tiniest smile. "Is there really a problem with my window? Or did you just finally decide to actually speak to me? Or, just stare at me a little closer?"

"Jesus. I'm so sorry. I didn't mean to stare. You're just..." Bren shook her head. "I'm an idiot. Yes, there's a crack in your window. I need to take a look at the inside, to see how bad it is."

The woman opened the door further and waved her in. "Do what you need to."

Bren ducked her head as she walked past and caught a whiff of the woman's smell. Fresh air and citrus. The apartment was lovely, but she already knew that. It was tidy, but not obsessively so. The painting she'd seen earlier had a sheet over it. "I'm sorry. I know you have company. I'll be quick."

She flinched almost imperceptibly at the mention of the older woman. "She's gone. You must have missed her when you were doing your circus trick down the building."

"Circus trick?"

"What would you call being strapped to something on the roof, so you can walk down the side of a building?"

"Rappelling? High-rise inspection? Sexy?" Bren wiggled her eyebrows and her stomach flipped when the woman laughed.

"Fair enough. I'm Jamie, by the way."

Bren started to hold out her hand, but turned away. Her

hands were filthy, and a flare of shame shot through her. "Bren. If I could just check the window, I'll get out of your head. Hair. I mean, I'll go away." She ran a hand through her hair. Smooth.

"I could make a cup of coffee? If you wanted to stay for a minute?"

Bren smiled. "I'd love that. But my partner is waiting for me at the truck. Rain check?"

Jamie looked so crestfallen Bren instantly regretted turning her down.

"Sure, of course. You're working. Another time—"

"Tomorrow? I'm off tomorrow. If you're free."

Jamie's smile was so beautiful it took Bren's breath away. "Tomorrow is perfect."

Bren quickly inspected the window. While most of the crack was outside, there was a hint of it that had come through. She frowned.

"Jamie, I'm sorry, but this has to be fixed as soon as possible. I can have some folks in tomorrow, and then maybe you and I could grab some lunch after?"

Jamie looked away, her expression pained, and she hugged herself. "I understand. But I can't leave...could we have lunch here?"

Bren nodded, wishing she knew Jamie well enough to take her into a strong hug, so much did she look like she needed one. "Of course. Sure. Here is fine too."

Jamie sighed in obvious relief. "Can you be here when they do the window, too? I'm not a fan of strangers."

"No problem. I'll be here around eight thirty, is that okay?"

Jamie's smile was like someone turning on the sun in a small room. The elevator doors slid shut and Bren took a deep breath. She felt like someone had turned on a tumble dryer in her stomach. Jamie was more beautiful than she'd thought, and the combination of humor and vulnerability was a heady mixture.

She met the window guys in the parking lot at seven thirty the following morning, not wanting them to go up to Jamie's without her. They rode up in silence, the guys obviously not in the mood for chitchat so early on a Saturday morning. The door slid open and Bren knocked.

They waited.

Bren knocked again, and the door was flung open. But it wasn't Jamie who opened it. The creepy older woman looked at them with undisguised irritation.

"Well? Come in. Fix it and get out."

"Yes, Ma'am. Bren Ryder." Bren held out her hand, challenging the woman to ignore her. The woman's return handshake was cold and limp, making Bren think of a dead fish.

"Jamie mentioned you'd been by yesterday." Her lip curled slightly like she smelled something off.

"Is she here? I'd like to discuss the process with her. Really, it would be better if she weren't here—"

"No! She does not leave this apartment. She has...special needs. She can't be bothered with the putrid outside world. She's far too delicate. Leave her alone, and do your job. She's fine."

The woman turned away and Bren had clearly been dismissed. She shook her head when one of the guys was clearly about to say something, and just waved them toward the window. She glanced at Jamie's closed bedroom door and sighed. The whole thing was off in a way she couldn't put her finger on. She turned her attention to the guys and waited as they discussed the best way to remove the window safely and replace it. The older woman sat in the dining room, a cup of something steaming in front of her, as she flipped idly through some fashion magazine.

Something moved in her peripheral vision and she saw Jamie's door open a crack, just enough for Bren to see her wide, frightened eyes. She motioned with a finger and Bren moved slowly toward the door in an attempt to keep from drawing the old woman's attention.

"Jamie? What's going on? Are you okay?" she whispered, keeping one eye on the dining room doorway.

"I can't explain now. Can you come back tomorrow? I'll be alone. Please? I need…just, please?"

Bren looked into Jamie's face and was baffled by the fear she saw. "Yeah, of course I can. I'll be here. Nine?"

Jamie nodded. "Whenever you want to come. I don't sleep much. Thank you."

She closed the door softly before Bren could say another word. Bren shook her head. What the hell had she gotten into? She had only taken a few steps when the old woman appeared in the doorway. "What are you doing? Get away from there."

Bren held up her hands. "I was just looking around. I was wondering what her painting was. I heard she's good."

The woman's head tilted slightly, and it reminded her of the way Jamie looked at her when she was checking the windows. Suddenly she wondered if the creepy woman was Jamie's mother.

"She is excellent. One of the best. Magical, really. Which is why she's so sensitive and must be left alone. And she certainly can't be around," she looked Bren up and down, "riffraff."

Bren felt her skin crawl. Anyone else and she would have given them some of their own attitude, but something about this woman was dangerous. Evil.

"No worries there, Ma'am. This riffraff knows where she belongs."

Bren turned away and supervised the rest of the window restoration. Although she glanced at Jamie's door throughout the morning, it never opened again. The old woman sat on the couch, an ominous deterrent.

By the time they left, Bren was exhausted, even though she hadn't really done anything. She and the guys left without a word, the old woman closing the door on them with a glare.

Bren broke out in goose bumps and one of the guys cleared his throat when the doors had closed.

"Creepy old cow," he said, and they all laughed, breaking the tension.

Something about Jamie called to her, and she felt, in some odd way, that she knew her. She jumped out of bed the next day, eager to get to Jamie's.

When she arrived, the receptionist wasn't at the front desk, but she saw the key card lying unguarded on the desk. She looked around, but the massive lobby was empty. She grabbed the card, raced to the elevator, and swiped it over the keypad. As the door began to slide shut she flung the key card back toward the desk and was satisfied when she saw it land at the base of the chair.

Once again Jamie opened the door before she knocked, and yet again she took Bren's breath away. A simple summer dress draped over her beautiful curves, her heavy crown of hair still in place.

"Good morning," she said shyly, looking down at her bare feet.

"Hey there. I was worried about you yesterday." Bren could have slapped herself in the head. Who opened with that with a total stranger?

"Thank you. It's been a long time since someone worried about me."

She led the way into the kitchen and Bren inhaled the smell of fresh coffee. The sun was rising over the city and the view was stunning. "Wow. Pretty amazing." She motioned toward the lightening sky.

Jamie looked at it thoughtfully. "It is. I've always wanted to see it from another vantage point though. Like the ocean. I'd love to see the sunrise over the ocean."

"You never have?"

Jamie handed her a cup of coffee and sipped her own, looking at Bren over the rim. "I'm sorry. I don't have much time, and I wanted to talk to you. Can I be blunt?"

Bren nodded and sat across from Jamie at the table. "By all means."

"Do you believe in magic? Do you believe in things you can't see?"

Bren considered the question carefully because she could see how serious Jamie was. "I do, in a way. I believe in ghosts, and in things that can't be explained away. I'm open to just about anything, really. I know there's evil in the world, so by that account, there must be good to balance it, right?"

Jamie let out a soft sigh and smiled. "I knew it. I knew you were the one."

"As much as I love hearing that, I'm a bit confused. I don't think you mean it the way other women have meant it." Bren winked to show she was kidding, and to lighten a moment that felt taut with possibility.

Jamie got up and went into the living room and Bren followed. Jamie pulled the canvas sheet from the painting she was working on and tossed it aside. "What do you see?"

Bren moved closer. "It looks like something out of a fairy tale. A woman locked away waiting for rescue, kind of thing." She turned toward Jamie. "Are you locked away? That woman…"

Jamie nodded, her shoulders slumped suddenly. "My mother. Kind of. She adopted me when I was a little girl. She came to the group home I was in, and she caught me…well, she saw me painting. But my paintings are different. I can make things happen in them. And when I change the painting, I can change the actual place." She looked up at Bren as though to gauge her reaction. "Look at the painting again."

Bren looked and nearly dropped her coffee cup. This time,

there was a figure on the side of the tower. And it looked like it was moving. Scaling the tower toward the woman at the top. "What the hell?" She leaned closer and could almost feel the breeze blowing the woman's hair. "How?"

Jamie shook her head. "I don't know. It's just part of me. But when Magna, my mother, saw me doing it, she wanted it. She brought me here, had me raised here by nannies until I could fend for myself. She comes and goes, thankfully. But I can't leave. She's done something to me, so that when I try to leave I panic. I get dizzy and scared and collapse before I can even get into the elevator."

Bren sat on the sofa and ran her hand through her hair, trying to grasp the situation. "So, you have some magical ability to draw paintings that change the world. And she uses that to, what, make money?"

Jamie nodded, her gaze searching Bren's.

"And you can't leave here because she's put some kind of spell or something on you?"

Again, she nodded but stayed silent.

"Does this have something to do with your hair? Is that why it's so long?"

Jamie laughed, but there was no humor in it. "Not really. She's convinced herself that I have to stay as much the same as I can, so that nothing changes my abilities. Which means not cutting my hair, and not going outside. Nothing can change, and nothing can influence. But when something comes to me, I have to paint. I can't *not* do it. And she knows that." She knelt down in front of Bren and took her hand. "But when I saw you, time after time, outside my window, I just knew you were going to be the one to help me. Do you know, aside from my mother you're the first person to step foot in this place in over ten years?" Her eyes welled up with tears and she held Bren's hand tighter. "Please help me."

Bren held the small, soft hands in her own and tried to think.

It was all so bizarre, but something about Jamie, and certainly the feelings she'd gotten from Jamie's mother, told her there was truth to it. Not to mention the figure still scaling the outside of the tower in the painting.

She stared outside, but her gaze drifted toward the newly placed window, which still had caution tape in front of it so no one leaned against it until it had completely set. She grinned as a plan formed in her head. "If we could get you outside, without the elevator, do you think you could get over whatever spell she put on you?"

Jamie's eyes grew wide. "You mean go down the side, like you do?"

"Yeah. I could go get my ropes and rigging, and rig one for you too. Then I could take you down the outside. Do you think it would work?"

Jamie walked to the window and looked down. Bren saw her clench her hands into fists. She spun around. "Let's do it. But you can't leave. We have to do it now."

"I don't have my rigging with me. I didn't think we'd need it for coffee, sorry." She smiled gently, but she could see a fire in Jamie's eyes.

"My hair is long enough, and strong enough, to get me to the next balcony. If we tie it up here, and you hold it steady and release it when I get there, you can come get me from the apartment below, right? I mean, they'd let me in, wouldn't they?"

Bren shook her head. "There's no one to let you in. That unit is empty. I can probably break in. But do you have any idea how crazy it sounds to let you go slinging yourself off a building using your hair? That's nuts."

Jamie's tears began to fall. "She'll know you've been here. She'll feel you. And she'll never leave me alone again. She'll hire someone to keep guard. This could be my only chance. Please. Please help me."

Bren couldn't withstand the onslaught of Jamie's tears and pleas. "Okay. Okay, fine. Can you get me a fine-edged knife of some kind? And a thick towel." Jamie got her the items she needed and Bren made quick work of the window, carefully undoing the thick rubber holding it in place and sliding it into the room. The open air this high up was invigorating and terrifying. She turned to Jamie and shrugged. "This is insanity."

"No more insane than the fact I've been locked in a tower all my life, waiting for you to come along." Jamie lifted her heavy hair and began unwinding the crown of it from her head. It lengthened and Bren was astounded at how long it really was. "What do I tie it to?"

Bren took the end of it and tied it around the Roman-type pillar in the middle of the room. Jamie stood at the edge of the window looking down. She gathered her hair around her hands, like a massive rope, and smiled at Bren. "See you downstairs."

She stepped off the balcony and Bren held tightly to the makeshift rope, letting it down slowly. It seemed like an eternity before Jamie shouted from below. Bren looked down and saw her standing on the balcony, her face flushed with excitement. Bren rushed back and unhooked her hair before taking the elevator to the correct floor. A few hard shoves with her shoulder and she was inside. She ran to the sliding door and let Jamie inside.

"Jesus. Are you okay?"

She held Jamie against her and felt like she'd been doing it all her life.

"I am. I'm okay!" Jamie looked stunned. "I'm free."

"Not yet you aren't. Do you need anything from upstairs? Any belongings or anything? ID? Cash?"

Jamie shook her head. "Bren, I don't have anything of my own. I don't really even exist outside those walls."

Bren took her hand and guided her out of the empty apartment. "We'll fix that. But let's get the hell out of here."

Together they entered the elevator and Bren kept her arm around Jamie, who pressed close to her, her hair gathered in a massive pile in her arms. When it opened into the lobby, the receptionist paled. "Ms. O'Cairn...your mother..."

They dashed past her and out to Bren's truck.

Bren turned the ignition and looked at Jamie. "Where to first, magic painter?"

Jamie took a deep breath and looked around her like a child. "Everywhere." She laughed, a clear, beautiful sound that made Bren's heart swell. "But first, I need a haircut." She leaned toward Bren and cupped her face. "I knew. I knew you were the one."

Bren covered Jamie's hand with her own. "Let's get you a haircut. And then we'll work on the everywhere part." She kissed the back of Jamie's hand and her lips tingled. "I don't know about magic, but I'm sure as hell glad you painted me into that picture."

Jamie looked out the window, her look faraway. "There are going to be lots more of those."

Bren pulled out of the parking lot. "Then we'd better get started."

# THE MILLER'S DAUGHTER

## Michael M. Jones

I came to her in her cell, just after nightfall.

I don't know what exactly I'd expected of Katharina, the miller's daughter. Perhaps a meek and terrified victim, reduced to tears by the sheer injustice of her circumstances. Perhaps a rage-weary firebrand, voice hoarse from shouting at her captors, nails bloody from scrabbling at the lock. Instead, I found a cool, calm, collected young woman, who prowled the confines of her quarters like an animal in a cage, examining it for weaknesses.

I think I fell in love with her a little in that moment.

Katharina was lovely in her own way. Her hair was long and fine, a silken blonde that tumbled down her back like a waterfall. Her eyes were a brilliant blue, sharp and intelligent. And her skin, with one exception, was smooth and lightly tanned from time spent outdoors. Were it not for the purple birthmark that stained her right cheek, she might even have been considered a great beauty, able to attract any number of suitors.

Alas, she had reached marriageable age and then some, with

no man able to overlook this flaw, despite her father's increas-
ingly outrageous offers of dowry. "It is but a fairy mark," he
claimed to all who would listen. "She was touched by the fairies
at birth, and imbued with a great gift, which will belong to
anyone who weds her." Had there been any fairies remaining in
our land to dispute this, they might have put to rest the claim
before it caused problems. But there were not, and they didn't,
and so it did.

The king had heard tales of Katharina, the miller's daughter,
who could spin straw into copper, silver, and gold. And the
king, a greedy man who never stopped to wonder why the miller
was not already wealthy beyond belief, took her for his own, but
with an ultimatum: Katharina would spin for him. If she passed
his tests, he would marry her and her father would be richly
rewarded. If she failed, there would be two new heads adorning
the spikes atop Traitors' Gate.

The king had no patience for failure.

I had no patience for the king, and so I came to Katharina
as night fell, appearing in the shadows of her cell with but a
whisper of cloak to herald my arrival.

I call it a cell, but it was a spacious tower chamber, bare
but for a few necessities...such as a spinning wheel and an
imposing pile of straw. There was a lovely view of Traitors'
Gate through the thin, barred window, to remind Katharina of
her fate should she prove inadequate. I was pleased to see that
it had not affected her.

She whirled when she sensed my presence, taking a step
back to eye me warily. I can only imagine what she made of
a hooded, cloaked figure, standing where none had been the
moment before. Remaining still so as not to spook her, I pushed
my hood back and let her look at me.

Slowly, she took in my own feminine features and long dark
curls, my red lips and dark eyes, my nonthreatening stance, and

she relaxed. Just a little. "Who are you?" she demanded. "Why are you here? If that bastard king sent you, tell him I can't work with an audience! The straw will turn to dust and he'll never have his riches and treasures."

My lips curled in a smile. Ash and oak, but I already admired her spirit. She had a fire that would be utterly wasted on the king. And yet, I had come to make sure she lived and ultimately married him. "Calm yourself, Katharina," I told her gently. "I know the truth of your supposed gift, and the fate that awaits you come the morning."

"Then why are you here?" she asked again, folding her arms sternly. "And just who are you?"

"I cannot tell you my name. But I'm here to help you. I will spin the straw into copper, enough for you to buy another day of life from the king."

As she assessed my offer, her eyes narrowed suspiciously. "And what will it cost me?"

That was the truth of it: favors never come for free in a world like ours. Debts must be repaid, scales balanced, obligations fulfilled. "Merely the ring you wear on your right hand."

She held her hand up to regard the simple emerald and silver ring, as though she'd forgotten it. "This? It's all I have to remind me of my mother. Surely, if you really can create gold out of straw, you don't need cheap baubles."

"True." I took her hand between mine—when had the distance separating us shrunk to almost nothing?—and she startled a little at the touch. Something stirred deep within me as I turned her fingers in my grasp. "It's worthless to me, but precious to you. And there must be a cost, Katharina. The ring—or your head on a pike."

She closed her eyes, inhaling and exhaling slowly. "The ring is yours if you do what you say you can do."

I ran my thumb against her fingers before releasing her. "So

be it." The back and forth of our bargaining verged on ritu-
alistic; it was invigorating and empowering, and new energies
ran through me, unlocked by the bargain's activation. "Sleep,"
I told her.

And she did, my magic caressing her as she fell into a deep,
restful slumber, curled up on the simple cot they'd supplied her.
I covered her with my cloak and went to work.

The job only took a few hours. When I was done, the pile of
straw had been replaced by copper. Coins and bars, ornaments
and knickknacks, fine pieces of jewelry and gaudy baubles.
Enough to please the king...for the moment. I knew this would
only whet his appetite. When I awakened Katharina, she stared
at my handiwork with a mixture of awe and fear, skepticism
replaced by newfound belief in my magical abilities. At the same
time, relief seeped into her, giving her a new measure of peace
that only enhanced her inner beauty. Her eyes shone a little with
unshed tears of joy, and I felt almost guilty as I held out my
hand for my payment.

She reluctantly dropped the ring onto my outstretched palm.
I slipped it onto my right hand. "This isn't the end of it, you
know," I told her. "I shall return when the king's greed over-
whelms his humanity."

"Wait," said Katharina. "Take me with you." It wasn't a
desperate plea; more a matter-of-fact suggestion, and again I
admired her focus.

I smiled sadly, shaking my head even as she spoke. "I cannot.
I am bound by rules, my dear. I can only free you if you guess
my name."

"How many guesses do I get?" she wanted to know. Oh,
canny girl. Asking the rules before leaping right into things.

"As many as you like," I said. "But I must be gone when
morning comes, and my visits are limited."

Katharina nodded. And for the remainder of the night, she

threw one name after another at me, every name she could think of, every name she'd ever heard. Each one was met by a shake of my head. For my name was not Abigail or Adele, Alexandra or Amelia. It was not Gertrude or Gisele, Ingrid or Irma, nor a hundred others. The morning came, and Katharina had not guessed my name. "I am truly sorry," I told her. I wrapped my cloak around me, and vanished into the shadows even as the sun's rays crept into the room, playing off the treasure trove of copper I'd left behind.

It was a week before the king's greed got the better of him and he once again locked his prospective bride in her cell with a daunting pile of straw and an unreasonable demand for silver. This time, when I appeared, Katharina was patiently waiting for me. She simmered with quiet anger and desperation, but her face was calm, her jaw set with determination. "You know what the king has ordered this time," she said.

"I do." I removed my cloak, draping it along the cot. Katharina's gaze followed me, studying me with an intensity that sent shivers down my spine, and desire racing through my bones. Oh, did she understand what that fierceness did to me? I wasn't sure; though there are those who would consider me quite fetching, with my lush curves and snow-white skin, with my regal features and remote demeanor, I had not thought Katharina the sort to seek the pleasures of a woman, especially a sorceress of unknown origin. But under her scrutiny, I felt oddly naked, despite the way my robes concealed so much of me.

Though thinking of those strong limbs wrapped around mine, that hair falling over bare skin, those lips tasting me— again, longing wove through me, leaving me wet and unsettled. It had been a long time since I'd taken a lover.

"You took my ring last time," she said. "I have no more possessions of value. You could have everything in this room, for all I cared."

"And because you care so little, I cannot accept that as payment." Suddenly, we were close—so close—to each other, her face inches away from mine. I was taller by half a head, and she tilted hers up to meet my eyes. I rested a hand on her cheek, covering the port-wine stain as with a lover's caress. My thumb gently stroked her skin. Her breath caught; her eyes half closed. "I will claim payment when my work is done," I whispered, my breath teasing her lips. "And you will give it freely."

"Yes," she whispered.

"Sleep." And she did.

And I worked. This time, when she woke, it was to the sight of silver everywhere. Coins and bars, plates and knives and goblets, bracelets and brooches. It was a king's ransom and then some; it shone in the moonlight that streamed through the window. Katharina gasped, overwhelmed by what she saw. As well she might have, for I had outdone myself in a desire to... impress her? Certainly, I cared not what that foolishly greedy king thought.

The look she gave me was almost heartbreaking. Could she feel the passion I'd poured into my creations? Could she sense how I felt about her, this brave, determined young woman? For we were kindred spirits, of that I had no doubt. Her breaths came quick and nervous as she waited to hear my price.

"A kiss," I told her.

"I've never been kissed," she confessed.

"I know." I cupped her cheek again, fingers gentle against the skin, and tilted her head to meet mine. Our lips came together in a soft moment of awkward fumbling before...

She responded with an endearing inexperience that spoke profoundly of hidden fire and repressed desire. Her lips parted at my subtle urging, and our tongues teased each other. I showed her the way, but she raced along the path like a wolf after a rabbit, threatening to leave me behind. Her fingers snuck into my hair, and I wrapped an arm around her waist to hold her close. When we finally broke apart, it was with heaving chests, mussed hair, and bruised lips. Her eyes were wide, almost fearful, and yet—she understood something new.

I smiled. "I find your payment...acceptable."

"Take me with you," she whispered hoarsely, less a cry for freedom and more a need to further explore these new and confusing emotions.

"Guess my name," I ordered her, even as I ran my hands over myself, making sure my clothes were in order again. Her eyes tracked my movements hungrily. I had to remind myself that she'd been starved for affection, lonely all her life, never desired in the way a woman should be desired. I could not let this go further tonight.

Until the sun came up, she made her guesses. But I was not Liesl or Leona, Michaela or Miriam, Theodora or Thora. And when the time came for me to go, it was with regret on both our parts.

This time, the king waited an entire month before succumbing to his base desires. This time, it was a veritable mountain of straw, enough to fill the chamber from floor to ceiling, and the demand was for gold.

This time, Katharina greeted me with a warm embrace that lasted too long to be friendly. I knew then that she had thought of me in my absence, and not just because I held the power to save her life. Did she dream of me, perhaps? Did she touch herself and wonder just how exactly I'd feel, taste, smell?

Oh, I had. Sex magic is very powerful stuff indeed, and in the depths of the forest I'd practiced the solitary arts in order to gather the power I'd need to perform tonight's miracle. I'd given myself to the earth, the wind, the night sky, the hidden pools. I'd stripped naked, spread my legs, plunged my hand between my legs, and fingered myself to screaming orgasms. I'd tugged at my nipples and raked my flesh, all for an imaginary lover who resembled Katharina in every regard. My arousal had soaked into the moss, the wind had teased away my scent, and the owls flew on my cries. The magic had infused me so I shone like the midnight sun, and I'd done it all for Katharina.

I pulled out of her arms to solemnly regard her. Her cheeks were flushed, her eyes bright, her lips slightly parted. She radiated excitement. "This will be my last visit," I informed her. "Three tests, three visits. We are all constrained by rules."

"I know," she murmured, her mood dimming at my straightforward manner. "And you will charge a hefty price indeed for this final miracle."

"I shall. But you will pay it."

She lowered her eyes, speaking toward the floor. "Gladly." Her tone was husky, just a little wanton; we both knew where this would lead. I knew on some level, she was willing to pay anything simply to survive. People are remarkably stubborn when it comes to defying fate, after all. I knew that in me, she saw survival and freedom. I knew that I'd awakened something long dormant within her.

Need.

Desire.

Lust.

I caressed her cheek, tipped her head up to again meet my gaze. I leaned in, my lips brushing hers. As she inhaled, I whispered: "Sleep."

And she did.

As Katharina, the miller's daughter, dreamed of freedom and the wild woods, I spun straw into gold and created such works as the world had never seen. I transformed her chamber into a place of luxury and decadence, where every stick of furniture, every trapping, every ornament, was spun from the finest of gold. I imbued it with warmth and softness, light and life.

The centerpiece of my labors was a great four-poster bed, as soft as a cloud with sheets finer than silk, pillows fluffier than any stuffed with goose down, and a near-transparent canopy. And on that bed I lay Katharina, and when all was ready, I woke her with a kiss.

She stretched and arched, fully rested, languid as a cat in a sunbeam, and gasped to see what I had wrought. "This is...I never could have imagined this," she breathed.

"All this, I've done for you," I said. "But now I shall claim my payment, and we will be quit. Scales balanced, obligations settled. The king will marry you. You will claim your gifts were exhausted by these trials; he will believe you and relieve you of any further tests. You will live long, have many children, and rule as a queen should. You will live...happily ever after."

My voice near broke on that last one. It was not a lie, but I knew she would not have a completely happy life with the king. Who could, knowing her husband would have killed her over something as ridiculous as copper and silver and gold? Foolish king. Katharina would have burned ever so brightly for anyone who simply loved her for herself.

She stared at me with those deep blue eyes, as if to read truth in my expression. I forced my features to remain still and stern. I started to reach for her—and then I stopped. I couldn't take that next step. I knew the price I wanted her to pay. So did she, I believed. We both paused for a long, long moment. My heart hammered in my chest, and I feared it would explode, or shatter into a million pieces. I swallowed my desire and loneliness and heartbreak down, and said, "I shall claim your firstborn as my own."

The sound she made nearly brought me to my knees; it was a cry of anguish and disappointment. I turned away so I didn't have to look at her. I wrapped my cloak tight around me, and took a step toward the shadows.

From behind me, a ragged plea. "Take me with you!"

I paused in mid-step. Without looking back, I replied, "Guess my name."

I was not Pauline or Petra, nor was I Reinheld or Rike. I was not Brunhilde, or Beata or Barbara. With each failed guess, I felt her come a little closer, until she was whispering names against my ear, her tone desperate and desirous. Her breath tickled the spot where neck met shoulder; I shivered even as my legs weakened and the moisture pooled between my legs.

Katharina kissed that spot, and I bit back the lightest of moans. She spoke a name, which I felt rather than heard.

"No," I told her. That was not my name. *Yes*, I thought. *Kiss me again.*

Her lips skimmed my neck. She traced another name with her tongue on my skin.

"No."

*Yes.*

She caught my arm, tugged until I twisted to face her.

She was naked. Every inch of smooth skin was on display, and I drank it in with hungry eyes. She was lean and lithe, well muscled and yet oddly delicate, surprisingly confident as she posed for me. My gaze swept over the curve of her hips, the swell of her breasts, the rosy nipples made taut with arousal. I noted the scarlet flush that crept down past her neckline, and the cascade of hair around her shoulders. As I watched, she lifted a hand to sweep the hair back, boldly displaying the stain on her cheek that had repelled so many suitors in the past, which had inadvertently gotten her into this predicament. She wore it now like a badge of honor, and she was radiant in her newfound boldness.

"Take me," she said. "If not as the price for your labors... then freely given while we still have this time. If you can't take me with you, then at least take me to bed." Her eyes glimmered with sudden tears. "If I must resign myself to a life with a king I despise, give me a night to last me a lifetime."

The pain in her voice—the naked longing and quiet resignation—finished the job of shattering my heart. But as she held her arms out to me, I felt the pieces already mending, renewed by something deep and strange. I could not save her from her fate—not unless she guessed my name, for there were rules binding us all—but I could grant this one last request.

Gladly. With all my repaired heart.

We came together in a sudden awkward tangle of limbs and lust, our mouths meeting in a hungry kiss, devouring each other with lips and tongue. Her hands fumbled at my robes; mine skimmed over smooth skin and lost themselves in golden hair. I cheated, exercising just a little of my unspent magic to let my clothes fall away in a shower of scraps, so many cloth petals to litter the floor at our feet. Katharina laughed against my lips at the odd sight, before renewing her efforts to explore me.

Oh, I was no beauty, not like her. I had some years on the miller's daughter, and more curves than was considered fashionable. It didn't matter to her. She found my breasts, cupping them in her hands, thumbs teasing the nipples to erectness with utter fascination. She was soft and warm and so very enthusiastic, filled with infectious joy, and I found my own reserve melting away.

I walked her backward, directing her with kisses and caresses, and we fell onto the golden bed in an awkward sprawl that took away our breath and left me on top. She lay under me, eyes wide with a wanton innocence that set fire to my nerves and left me dripping with need. The need to please her, to claim her, to know her completely.

And I did. With fingers and mouth, I taught Katharina, the miller's daughter, the ways of women together. I kissed my way over her breasts, down her stomach, and between her legs. I spread her with my fingers, and buried my face in her sex. I stroked the length of her, tasting her wetness, teasing her with the flicking of my tongue and the warmth of my breath. As Katharina moaned, whimpered, and clenched handfuls of golden sheets, I drank my fill of her. I tormented her to the brink of orgasm with my mouth...and then I fucked her with my fingers. I alternated in this fashion until she exploded with pleasure, crying inarticulately, shuddering over and over while the aftershocks rippled through her body.

Then it was her turn to demonstrate what a quick learner she was. She kissed me fiercely, licking her taste from my lips with utter fascination, before encouraging me to lie back so she could explore me. For what felt like hours, she stroked and caressed me, listening to my moans and murmured instructions—yes, there, more, harder, yes, don't hesitate—working me into a right state of arousal indeed. My nipples grew painfully tight, and I pinched them for relief even as she took her first taste of my sex.

The hesitant, feather-soft touch of tongue on clit nevertheless felt like lightning; I arched and commanded her to continue. She paused as if to savor me, as if to decide that she liked what she'd found, and then, awkward and inexperienced but oh so eager to learn, she devoured me. I looked down, and there was that golden waterfall of hair, falling over my thighs; it was a sight I'd never forget, nor grow weary of.

If only we weren't bound by rules.

As I orgasmed, magic escaped from me, bathing the room in sparkles and vivid colors, fading away slowly as I returned to my senses and reclaimed control. Stray magic twisted around us like dust motes in the sunlight, reminding me that time still ticked on and our long night would end sooner than we liked.

Determined to give Katharina as much satisfaction as possible, I pulled her into my arms, claiming her mouth with mine in another needy kiss. I breathed in her scent, fixing it in my memory. I would take her with me in spirit, if nothing else. I teased her with my fingers, and once more she opened herself to me. Soaked, hot, tight, arching into my touch desperately. I stroked and rubbed, feeling the tension build within her. I—

I couldn't let it end so simply.

"Say my name," I whispered.

Katharina moaned, unable to put together coherent syllables.

"Say my name," I repeated, several fingers thrusting faster to match her ragged breathing.

She mumbled something, begging me for more, more, more.

"Say my name," I demanded, my hand moving furiously as she ground herself against the merciless onslaught of sensations. "Katharina the miller's daughter, if you love me... Say. My. *Name!*"

And as the orgasm tore through her, so did my secret name rip itself from her parted lips, a nonsense collection of sounds which defined me, gave me form and function and power and meaning, which bound me and limited me.

Her cry freed me to act as I would. To raise my magic and break the invisible chains which locked us into our roles. To snip unseen threads and shatter unknown locks. As the sun rose outside Katharina's cell, I carried us both away with the bed itself in a swirl of golden wind, far from greedy kings and foolish fathers.

In our wake, all the copper and silver and gold I'd spun for the king turned to dust and cobwebs. He would not benefit from my labors, nor profit from his greed ever again. He would die in a hunting accident before taking a wife; the throne would pass to a far wiser cousin who would rule with grace and dignity. The miller would one day receive a message stating that Katharina was happy and cared for and no longer his concern. He would live well, but deep in his heart, he'd regret the foolishness that cost him his daughter.

Elsewise and elsewhere, Katharina and I lay curled together in my own decidedly non-golden bed, speaking of life, love, and the future. We spoke of learning magic and defying propriety and living happily ever after.

"And," she said with a soft laugh, "to think you wanted my firstborn." She rolled over to kiss me playfully. "I give you that as well, willingly, however it might come about."

"What service shall I perform to earn that payment?"

"I'm sure we can find something…"

And we did. For many years to come.

# WARRIOR'S CHOICE

## A. D. R. Forte

Another tourist attraction in the impatient midst of the bustling, honking downtown, the palace dreams its dreams. They have pulled down the old ruins of the walls now, and anyone can get to the gardens, a shrubby fragment of their former glory. But it was not always this way.

Once, the walls towered, crowned with iron spikes. Once, only the faintest scent of roses wafted out into the night. Borne by the wind. Blown by the breath of a princess.

She leans her head against the window arch, letting the night cool the ache and heat of the revelry below. A few precious minutes of escape. A respite from excess, from glittering, smiling duty. She lifts a hand to her head, to the confection of gold mesh and filigree birds with eyes of jewels. It is heavy, this towering artistry of the hairdressers' guild, and it weighs on her neck with the burden of an iron ring. It cages more than her dark hair.

She would tug at the coif, send the birds flying to a watery grave in the fountains far, far below. If she dared. But she cannot. No more than she can forever say, "No." To her father. To the state. To the bonds of birth.

But she can reach her arms to the distance that unfolds beneath her, away from her, into a destiny she cannot imagine. She can sing of all she cannot say, of all she cannot even think, to the night wind that carries her song across the plains and out into the wide world, to fall where it may.

Maevyn wakes, shivering in her furs. The stars are bright pinpoints in the darkness, but their light is not what has wakened her. Nor is it the cold, though her breath turns to steam as she gets to her feet and reaches for bow and knife. Snow mutes her footsteps and pine branches brush, sharp and pungent, by her face until she reaches the wooden bridge where the river churns, still and sluggish, between its banks.

In this season, there is no travel. The Hadrai huddle close to their fires, within the shelter of stone and wood. The warriors take their skills to the foothills in search of meat, and even they share the fires of the small folk when they can. As she does now, following the sound of pipes to the vale below. There is a song playing in her head, but not one of the folk. Not a song of the Hadrai. Not one she's ever heard before.

And yet it goes on, a ripple of notes so exquisitely joined they might almost hide the sorrow in the melody, the loneliness in this song she doesn't know. The call that drives her to search for something, somewhere, against all good common sense.

"Who is it that calls?" says a voice in the dark.

"It is I," she replies as she steps into the edge of the fires' glow.

"Maevyn. And how fare you?"

She nods her head at the small, gray-bearded man, but in the way of his kind, he senses what she doesn't say. He holds out a pitcher and mug, gestures to the nearest fire ring.

"Come," says he, "and tell me what disquiets your soul."

If only she could. If only there were a way to describe this nameless, faceless longing. This compulsion, this knowledge that she must *go*. Though to do so is madness. And folly.

"If the wind calls to you," says the wise man, "you know you must follow it. The wind never speaks for nothing."

If only it would tell her: *Why her?* If only it would tell her what path it wants her to travel.

Before first light, she leaves the valley and the mountains dreaming in the last stillness of winter night.

*I go*, she thinks, *to almost certain death*. But surely the wind cannot be so capricious, so devious. Instinct tells her the trail she follows is not false, and she believes it, though everyone has judged her insane.

"But where do you go?" Commach has asked. No, demanded, as he thinks he has a right to. And with a stifled sigh, she has, out of kindness, tried to explain. The expanses of land flat as a pancake, jeweled with rivers and great swaths of water. Like lakes, but so flat. Not even a hillock in sight. Buildings and walls of towering, golden stone, sprawling in every direction. Sand and dust everywhere the rivers and strange lakes don't touch. A land for giants.

*West*, the wind seems to whisper. West, where nothing lies but frost and impassable peaks. But perhaps beyond the peaks. What then?

Commach has turned away in disgust, not bothering for the first time to try to touch her hand. To boldly brush his shoulder against hers. Realizing at last that his bid is lost. *You go to your death.*

And maybe she does. She hasn't told Commach or anyone about the flowers. Red like blood, ringed by thorns. But beautiful, so beautiful. Petals soft as fur. She aches to touch them, willing to brave the thorns, to bleed on them for the chance to breathe their sweetness, to rest her skin against silken blooms. Maybe that will be her demise.

In the logic of dream, such a death seems worth it.

In a story, she might have been bewitched, sad and fading under the curse of some ruthless enemy of the state, some deity jealous of her beauty but unable to destroy it. In reality, she has the morning attendants powder her cheeks to restore their glow, line her eyes with charcoal to hide the red cast of sleepless nights. She herself paints on her smile, draws on her gracious hands and more gracious nods. The suitors come and they go. She dismisses them with quiet words. If she laughs without mirth, why, no one hears the difference.

In a story, heroes and champions might come from far and wide to discover the cure to her mysterious sorrow, to win her hand for the feat. Alone at her window, where no one knows her pain, she gives her songs to the wind that seeps through the gardens and over the lakes, carries the scent of the roses and the notes of the song out across the desert. To whatever lies beyond.

In a tent under desert stars, Maevyn lies awake, waiting for the wind. Sometimes it's a useless effort, and the wind is nothing but a harsh, destructive demon, burying men and beast under the pitiless sand. But there are the times when it's not. Tonight, it's soft as a veil of silk.

She opens the tent flap and the wind steals in with gentle touch, not yet bitterly cold, but no longer singed by the day's fierce heat. It caresses her unbound hair, tugs at the loose nomad shirt she wears. It sweeps around her, singing of longing, of loneliness, and the perfume of the roses fills the tent. She has a word for them now, the fierce, red blooms, but their thorns still haunt her sleep.

The traders and caravan guards that she makes her way with

now cannot help her with the roses. They shake their heads and fold their arms into their sleeves. "The roses only grow at the royal palace," they say, and look at each other and quickly at their shoes. They have never been to the palace. It is not for folk such as them. *It is not for strangers, barbarians either.*

They have given her space in their camps, a place for her long-sword and knife to earn passage with them. Even a command, a company of mercenaries both grizzled and green who, willing or grudging, will yet do what she says. They have slept and starved with her across these many months, forgiving her Hadrai ignorance, her strange manners and stranger skin. But their palace they guard with mulish resolve.

The wind goes, as suddenly as it has come, leaving her empty and aching, kneeling at the edge of the tent. She reaches up a hand to call it back, force it, will it to stay. *Tell me why.*

But it doesn't return. And in the morning, she marshals her troops, standing chill as the morning while she waits. She *will* go to the palace, no matter what they say. In that, she has no choice. In that, she follows fate.

Hand raised against the golden warmth of the sinking sun, she comes to the window, to the view that doesn't change, insensible to months and years. Insensible to time and age. She no longer sings of sorrow. She no longer sings from pain.

The suitors no longer come and go. She doesn't have to smile through silent screams of rage. But she has traded a gown for a robe, the politics of the ballroom for the courts of law. Her father sniffs with approval, if not content, and they marvel at her wisdom, at her justice, at her knowledge for one so young.

If only they knew her for a fool. She has but changed one duty for another, and bound by duty still, she remains.

Then, as if it has just remembered a forgotten task, a neglected errand, a breath of wind steals by and touches her cheek. It flutters the edges of her long, severe robe, brings with it the cool breath of oasis flowers, the warm dust of horse hooves, the patter of rain on a lake. Her heart suddenly aches, and tears long dry sting her throat.

She shivers, but she throws the robe back, lets the sunlight wash over her bare skin. In drowsy waves, the scent of roses wafts up from the gardens below, and she abandons herself to the caress of the wind, the sun, and the roses. She sighs gently into the swirling currents of air as her nipples tighten and her sex pulses with need.

Flushed and gasping, she catches herself with one hand against the window arch, and stares out across the world. To distant roads that wind their slow way across the state, to the palace at its heart. The hooves of a horse fly beneath her, the world a blur through which she speeds. She urges the horse to fly faster, to ride the wings of the wind itself. So long. *So long I've waited.*

She has no breath to sing, but she cries out. A sound of raw, primal longing. Echoing. Reverberating. She lets the power of her need flow out and away.

She rides into the city as the sun falls away. Kyre-Maevyn, they call her now. Captain. Master of the Blade. Gold clinks heavy enough in her purse for even the finest inns, warm light and rest and shelter and deference to one who wears the cloth of the Imperial Blades. From the darker, dirtier streets, other temptations materialize in doorways: painted lips and nipples, knowing hands and mouths.

But she passes it all like a shadow in the night. She knows only impatience. She leaves behind the streets and the crowds, wends her way up. To the center of the city where the palace lies.

She has served in the farthest outposts, where new recruits and commoners and foreigners serve. In barracks tenanted with rats. Eating gruel and chopping wood, slopping out the filthy backwaters of the state. She has imagined the horrified look on Commach's face if he were to see her so fallen, digging ditches at the order of fat, provincial governors, and it has made her smile. For this she has done by choice.

*No barbarian will ever wear the cloth of a Blade. No woman will ever wield a Captain's longsword.* But she has proven them wrong.

They don't know she hasn't had any other choice.

And now at long last, the palace gates will open to her, admit her past the impossibility of the walls. She doesn't go to the quarters appointed to her in the Kyre-fas. She hands sword belt and bag to a page and lingers in the common room of the fas for a while, nursing a cupful of wine, ignoring the spiced bread and meat laid out on the long, white tables. Listens idly to the chatter of tipsy guards and drunken Blades, the rattle of dice, the hum of a guitar from some hidden corner. While beyond the pillars of the hall, the wind pines and frets, bringing her the scent of roses. Close, so close. So very, very close now.

No one notices when she rises, slips between the shadows of the pillars and out into the dark. She doesn't have the measure of the palace, the paths and the steps and terraces that divide its mazelike, sprawling width. But she doesn't hesitate all the same. She walks with feverish urgency along the unfamiliar path, following the pull of desire and the promises of the wind, trusting her steps to fate.

They meet in the scented night, within the shadow of the garden walls. The rose bushes grow high against the stone, supple branches heavy with blossoms, leaves rustling whispers in the night. A secret, wanton arbor where the captain falls to her knees before the princess, who waits lovely and still as the molded statues that grace the fountain gardens.

"Princess," Maevyn says, hoarse with the effort to find words after so long. After an age of waiting and aching and following a dream to the reality of lust. After all, she will not meet her death. At least, not in the way of the warrior. She bends her head in supplication, in passion, in the sweetness of surrender.

"You are forbidden," the princess whispers. Her fingertips raise Maevyn's chin up, draw loose the bands that hold back the folds of Maevyn's hair. She shivers as she lets it flow over her hands.

"You have called me."

She undoes the lacings of Maevyn's tunic, slips her hands between the leather folds.

"You break the rules of the state."

Maevyn writhes under her touch, nipples pinched into violent need.

"At your wish," she gasps, but it is all she can say. Her hands, browned and scarred by wind and blade, reach out, grasping for anchor in this tossing sea of sudden, mindless desire.

The princess's hips are soft, curved like the giant bell that hangs in the mountain hall of the Hadrai chief. They yield to her grip, rolling with voluptuous promise as she pulls down, as the princess falls back beneath her, legs parting under the force of Maevyn's knees. The princess laughs and spreads her legs wider.

"You violate me," she says.

"Yes."

The fabric of the judge's robe rips, no match for a warrior's strength, and Maevyn discards the torn fabric like a fragment of night, leaves the princess bare and unmasked. She closes her eyes as Maevyn's lips open hers, and her hands punish again. Finding Maevyn's breasts, squeezing the tender flesh, nails scoring skin, thumb and forefingers tightening beyond the limits of even a warrior's pain. For this is not the pain of the battlefield. Love devastates as battle never can. Maevyn cries out into the kiss, sex pulsing with torment and need, and the princess releases her nipples to heat and agony, pushes her tunic away.

Bare skin falls on bare skin, bodies crushed together in embrace. The princess's tiny cruel teeth find her neck, nip and pull at undefended skin, and Maevyn thrusts her rough hands between untouched, delicate thighs. Feels the princess arch and hears her half-stifled cry.

*My hands to serve her*, she has vowed. The words of the Imperial Blades. With a single finger, she parts the princess's wet folds, circles the tip of her sex. A shudder and another cry as reward. Maevyn smiles as she pushes even deeper, into her princess's innermost folds. Her princess forgets to bite, forgets that she ought to be punishing her errant Blade. She only clings and quivers as Maevyn slides fingers, now gentle, now rough, deep into her and then out again, teasing her wet sex, rubbing it hard. She sobs with pleasure as Maevyn moves her head to one lush breast, captures the nipple with her tongue, licking it, suckling it, as her fingers carry out their dance. Inside and out, slick now with passion. Relentless in their fury.

Her princess will be sore, rubbed raw, by the morning. She will feel it with every solemn step, as she makes her way to the courts, to the thrones, as she passes high above the training yards and barracks of the Blades. Maevyn smiles around the nipple in her mouth. The unanswered torture between her own legs is intolerable. It pierces her with every motion, demanding to be addressed. But this is the wind's cruel promise. The thorns of the rose that bleed her of breath.

The princess cries out and clenches her legs, but still Maevyn takes her, not allowing any reprieve. And the scent of the roses seems to deepen. The princess shudders and shudders in her arms. Maevyn lifts her head to draw her lips across moist and shivering skin. Finds the princess's panting mouth and savages her waiting lips. Their tongues meet, twine like mating snakes, struggle against each other. Subside.

The wind brushes over their bodies, cooling the sweat of their exertions, evening and calming their ragged breath. Frenzy fades into stillness.

They wait in the dewy garden for the coming of daybreak when they must return to their fates. But the bonds of duty weigh lighter now under the hidden bindings of bliss. Under the secret promise of nights to be.

"I would go with you if I could," she says with her head on Maevyn's shoulder. "To the cold mountains of the East."

She turns and lifts a hand, strokes delicate fingers along Maevyn's cheek.

"Instead I keep you in exile here, for my pleasure."

Maevyn catches her hand and kisses each finger. Smiles at the way it makes her princess shiver.

"By my choice," she says.

# TROLLWISE

## Sacchi Green

Trip, trop, trip, trop. Hjørdis stood back in disgust as Princess Tutti pranced across the bridge, hips swaying, the false tail strapped to the seat of her gown twitching. A coy toss of Tutti's head knocked the goat horns on her headdress slightly askew. "Oh, Mr. Troll," she piped in a falsetto voice, "are you there today? Don't you want to eat us up? Look, this time there is a meatier prey than just we little goats!" She cast a mocking glance back toward Hjørdis. "A buxom brood mare!"

Hjørdis would have swatted the silly girl's rump if there had been enough of it to be worth the trouble. Or, more truthfully, if she herself had not been bound by oath to abide peaceably among these puny southerners. For now. As it was, she took a threatening stride onto the wooden planks. Tutti ran off giggling toward the meadow, from which sounds of pipes and laughter and occasional playful shrieks rose above the lazy burbling of the stream.

Princess Vesla, also adorned with horns and tail, came up timidly beside Hjørdis. "There truly was a troll under the bridge a week ago," she said in a tremulous voice. "When Tutti called out, I heard his voice, like the rumbling of stones. She thinks it was Werther, the dancing master, trying to frighten us, but I'm sure it wasn't!"

"Oh? What did he say?" Hjørdis made some small effort to tolerate Vesla, who was not so spiteful as her sister Tutti. She felt also a slight sympathy for the girl, who had formed a hopeless passion for Hjørdis's captive brother Harald. At least accompanying them on their outing, however nasty it promised to be, was an excuse to leave the castle.

"He said, 'Scrawny bones not fit to pick my teeth! Get you gone!'" Vesla shivered. "But we haven't heard him since."

Hjørdis knew a great deal more about trolls than these little twits ever could. More than anyone could who had not known Styggri. That sounded all too much like what Styggri *would* say, in a humorous mood. But Styggri had crossed into another world from which there was no return.

Hjørdis looked more closely at the bridge. Its sides and the pillars beneath were stone, with wooden planking wide enough for two carriages to pass side by side over its double arch. And wide enough for a troll to lurk beneath, although why one should wish to, or venture this far south at all, was beyond her. Still... She gazed far upstream to where water surged out from a cleft in a rocky hillside. Nothing to compare with the jagged mountains and plummeting rivers of her home, but still part of a long arm of hills and ridges reaching out from those same mountains.

"You go on to your frolicking." She gave Vesla as gentle a shove as she could manage. Gods, these pampered southern girls were brittle, twiggy things! And their brother the prince— her husband under duress—was no better. "I'll sit a while here in the shade of the birches. This heat annoys me."

"Oh! Are you, then...already..."

"No! And if I were, it would be too soon to know. Go along now!"

Vesla went, trying to keep the gilded wooden heels of her shoes from making as much noise on the bridge as Tutti's had done. Once safely across she looked back over her shoulder. "Give Werther a few stomps from me," Hjørdis called. The foolish dancing master deserved whatever he got, with his tales of ancient times in foreign lands where satyrs danced on goat hooves and bands of women ran wild under the spell of a wine god.

It had all got somewhat garbled. Tutti had stuck various bits together, so that now the weekly game was for the ladies to pretend to be goat-like satyrs and trample on whichever courtiers and servants were willing to prostrate themselves in the meadow grasses, which turned out to be a surprising number, including, of course, Werther himself. Vesla had said wistfully that she wished Harald were allowed to join them, at which Hjørdis had snapped that if her brother were fool enough to submit to such atrocities, she would abandon him to his fate, vow or no vow.

Tutti had hinted that even Prince Oleg might be there today. All the more reason for Hjørdis to stay away. Let her husband take what pleasures he might, since thus far he had been unable to take pleasure in her.

Her marriage to the king's son had been the ransom demanded for Harald, and even then he would not be released until she had provided a strong grandson of the king's blood as heir to the kingdom. The marriage vows meant nothing to her, being made before gods not her own, but her personal vow to redeem her brother was a matter of honor. At least she had won the release of the crew that had sailed with him in search of adventure and, of course, of the girls over the next hill, or past the farthest fjord, or in distant lands, who always held the promise of being more beautiful than the willing girls at home.

Prince Oleg, however, had not yet managed to live up to his half of the arrangement. Hjørdis had tried, in good faith, to be gentle and not loom over him if she could avoid it, but he still trembled when they were alone together, and, though he was clearly aroused, he could not keep from shrinking away at her touch.

Hjørdis knew she was no beauty, but she had never lacked for suitors, and it was not merely that her father's great mead-hall above Hardangerfjorden claimed the allegiance of Jarls over a vast territory, or that she herself would inherit lands high in the mountains from her mother's brother. Her body was lush as well as strong, with much to offer beyond the promise of tall sons. If there was no man to whom she wished to offer it, all the better now that duty left her no choice.

The true choice of her heart had never been possible. Still, she had known two summers and a winter of great joy, more than many people were granted in their lifetimes. And the high mountains were still there, beyond the Trollveggan massif, even if Styggri was gone from them these five years now. Once her vow was fulfilled, Hjørdis would leave this flat land, leave even the child, which would doubtless be taken from her in any case. Better not to think of that. Better to be lulled by the voice of the water, close her eyes and see the mountain home of her memories.

At first, when the voice of the water changed, that too seemed a mere echo of those memories. The longer her eyes remained closed, the longer she could imagine that Styggri was there, moving through the stream...climbing the bank...circling to stand behind her in the utter silence only a troll could manage... and Hjørdis felt a sudden presence like an unseen shadow cast across her. A troll, some troll, stood there.

"Good day, Elder Cousin." Hjørdis spoke the formal greeting

in the ancient troll tongue, as she had been taught by her uncle. Whether the trollfolk were truly distant kin of mankind, as they might well be, there was no denying that they had followed the retreating ice high into the mountains long before her own people had arrived. And more than likely that many a family had traces of troll blood in their background.

"You do not cross the bridge?"

Not a voice like the rumbling of stones at all. Closer to the murmur of fine gravel sifted through their fingers when they had searched together for blood-red crystals of garnet, like the silver-wrapped pendant that hung between Hjørdis's breasts. Not Styggri's voice as it had been when she was young, in the Huldra form, able to be-spell men...and Hjørdis...with her song; yet it *was* her voice.

Hjørdis could not bring herself to turn and look. Hope leapt, then wavered, weighed down by disbelief, even a shiver of dread. *In five years you would not know me*, Styggri had said, *even if I returned from under the mountains and did not cross over into the ice world.* And Hjørdis had known it to be true. Troll women lived long, but left youth and any fleeting grace or beauty behind quickly. There were fewer and fewer of the troll-kind left, even high in the mountains, and all she had known until Styggri had seemed very old indeed, including Styggri's mother.

She must look, soon, but first she spoke. "There is nothing across the bridge for me."

"Your prince is there."

"No one of mine is there. No one of mine is still in this world, or so I was made to believe."

Another spell of silence. Then, in the day-to-day speech of the mountain Norsemen, easier for them both, Styggri said, "I came back after all, and found you had gone off to wed a king's son."

Hjørdis's neck was stiff from the effort of not turning. She stood and swung around in a single motion. "How can I know you are not a shade, an illusion, a snare?" But she did know. The deep-set gray-green eyes, shadowed now by thicker brows and creased at their corners, were still clear as mountain pools. The hair, even paler than it had been, arched back from a thong cinched high on her head, a traditional style seldom seen now even among the oldest trolls. Her nose was more pronounced, her face broader than it had been, and so was her body, arms and legs heavily muscled as was the way with trollkind, male or female. In elk-hide breeches and loose wool tunic she could have been either, to a casual observer.

"What would you take as proof?" Styggri's face remained carefully expressionless.

Hjørdis moved forward until the fine velvet of her gown brushed the homespun wool. She had been the taller by a little when they were younger; now they stood nose to nose. Slowly she bent her head, pressed her mouth to the hollow of Styggri's throat, and drew her tongue along exposed skin that shivered at her touch. "Taste does not lie."

She raised her head. The wide smile on Styggri's face was the final proof. Years rolled away. They might have been lying on the sunlit rock beside a reed-edged mountain stream where Styggri had first spoken those words.

Hjørdis had followed Harald that day only because he was so determined not to be followed. Whatever drew him must be worth seeing, since he had at last stopped pining for the fjords and his dragon ship and his friends, and the girls at home, as he'd done throughout the visit to their uncle's domain. It must have something to do with a girl, though. She'd seen him out past the cattle byre last night with the cowherd, their expressions and gestures and rough laughter reeking of lascivious intent.

The fellow must have told him where to find some particularly tempting morsel.

It was easy enough to keep out of Harald's sight, especially since Hjørdis wore a pair of his brown leggings rather than her own skirt. She could move upslope and down, from boulder to boulder, with far more ease than her seafaring brother. She was at home here in ways that he was not, which was why her uncle had decreed that she should inherit his lands and responsibilities when the time came.

Harald crested a ridge and stood, enthralled, before starting down into the stream-carved vale that Hjørdis had thought of as her own personal retreat. From the look on his face it was not the stream spreading out into a little marsh that drew him, nor the waterfall from which it flowed, nor the reeds and wild-flowers, nor the dense growth of spruce on the slope beyond with tender new growth at the tip of each branch so brilliant a green it looked like a host of tiny flames.

No, it was some woman. Some brazen, naked woman, she saw, when, forsaking stealth, she reached the ridge top. By then Harald wouldn't have noticed if she'd hurled stones at him, as she was sorely tempted to do. Or at the woman, scarcely more than a girl, reclining on the sunlit rock where Hjørdis liked best to sit.

Slim, seductive, long-legged, with pale hair streaming past her exquisite face over her shoulders and across breasts that peeked in and out between the flowing tresses; surely this was an illusion born of Harald's fantasies! And, Hjørdis had to admit, of her own.

Then the girl tilted back her head, gazed up at them both, opened her lovely mouth, and sang. The clear, high sound flowed over Hjørdis, piercing her body, pulsing in her veins. An illusion indeed, an enchantment out of the storied past, when there was magic in the world far beyond what little remained. When troll girls in the Huldra form enticed men with their songs, enslaved them, making them forget all else.

Harald, besotted, charged down the slope, stumbling, falling, rising, lurching forward, compelled by the song and the promise of that enticing body.

A surge of rage saved Hjørdis from just such madness. The song, the allure, the enchantment; none of it was meant for her! Never for her! She stood on the height, glaring down upon them like an avenging Valkyrie even as she shook inside with a longing as fierce as her anger. Let the seductress do as she would with him! Let her...

But as Harald stumbled again, just short of his prize, the girl vanished. When he looked up there was nothing to see but empty rock. He searched all around in a frenzy of thwarted desire, thrashed through the reedy marsh, peered into the stream as though she might have swum away like a mermaiden.

Hjørdis descended without hurry. "Go on home," she told her brother. "You look like you've seen a ghost. The air this high in the mountains can have that effect on those not suited to it." Harald was not convinced, but neither was he about to tell his sister what he'd been hoping for, though the persisting bulge in his trousers was evidence enough. He stomped off, sulking, and by the top of the ridge he was breathing as hard as though the air was indeed too thin for comfort.

Hjørdis perched on the edge of the rock. When she was quite sure Harald was gone, she said calmly, "You might as well come out now." There was a long bulge in the stone that had not been there yesterday. Stones did not grow overnight. Besides, Hjørdis had had a better view of what transpired than Harald.

The hard surface shimmered for a few seconds, and then a shape emerged. Not so slim or long-legged now, with a round, laughing face that, while scarcely fairy-tale perfect, did possess a certain charm. To Hjørdis the sturdy naked body was just as alluring as the one seen through the haze of illusion, but she had no intention of revealing her vulnerability. "I can't say much for your taste in men," she said coolly.

The girl sat up and shrugged. "There is so little entertainment here. And are you certain it was he I sang for?"

Hjørdis's brows arched in skepticism even as something lurched inside her. Then she frowned and looked more closely. "I should know you. You're the healer's girl Styggri, aren't you? Old Hilgra's? But you were just a small child..."

"No smaller than you! And I did not hide behind my mother's skirts, while you always hung back behind your uncle."

Even that long ago they had eyed each other with as much challenge as curiosity. Hjørdis had been taken to the troll healer several times over the years to learn the simpler skills of herbal healing that she might need as Lady of her uncle's Hall, but Styggri had seldom been present, and not seen at all for several years. Now Old Hilgra was gone as well.

"Your mother..." Hjørdis paused. None knew for sure whether the healer had died or simply moved on.

"Gone to another place. As I have been, studying troll lore." She stopped abruptly, as though she had said more than she ought, then went on, "I've returned to be healer for the few of trollkind still here, but I must leave again in two years."

Hjørdis, too vividly aware of Styggri's casually naked body, kept a stern hold on herself. "So is lounging about wantonly like this..." she gestured along the sprawling form, "any way for the healer to behave?"

"Was bathing naked in the stream yesterday any way for the future Lady of the Hall to behave?" Styggri's impudent grin was triumphant.

"It was you moving behind the spruce boughs! I thought some small animal was browsing." Hjørdis was startled, but not entirely displeased.

"I saw. And afterward I let that cowherd view me briefly, in hope that he would spread the word, and you might come, and I could test whether my song worked on a woman as well as a man." She raised one leg and let it lie negligently across Hjør-dis's lap.

Hjørdis pretended to ignore it, though her lap was all too aware of the tantalizing pressure. She hoped the heat rising through her body was not too evident on her face. "So now you've played your little game, and lost."

"Do you forget that a healer must know all the ways of the body?" Styggri moved up to straddle Hjørdis, pressing her round breasts against Hjørdis's own, covered only by a thin linen shirt. "I do not think that I have lost."

Hjørdis did not think so, either, but by the goddess Freya, she would not admit to it. No matter that the scent of Styg-gri's body, mingling with that of wildflowers and sun-warmed spruce needles, sent desire racing through her veins like those of any spring-crazed creature. She stared into the troll girl's brook-green eyes with all the stern challenge she could muster. "I will not be toyed with!"

"No?" Styggri slid her hands up under Hjørdis's shirt to cup her breasts, which certainly did enjoy being toyed with; then, too soon it seemed, she removed one hand to work it down deep, deep into the borrowed leggings. A shudder of pleasure rose all the way to Hjørdis's hairline, though she kept her gaze on the other's round face, and managed to stifle a whimper of disappointment when the fingers were slowly withdrawn.

Styggri raised a finger to her mouth and licked at it. "Taste does not lie," she said, and slid the finger into Hjørdis's mouth. It was not the first time Hjørdis had tasted her own arousal, but never on any hand but her own. No, her taste did not lie.

"If you are to demonstrate more...more of how much a healer knows of the body"—she could scarcely speak coherently—"we'd best move out of sight of any cowherd or bull-brained brother who might return." They both looked toward the little waterfall, then at each other, realization dawning that the small cave screened by flowing water each had thought her own private hideaway was not so private after all. That in itself seemed nearly as powerful a bond as their shared lust.

A pair of white gyrfalcons circled high overhead, calling shrilly to each other, but once shielded behind the quivering wall of water no sound from outside could reach the girls. They could scarcely hear themselves at first, until it became a game to see who could force the most extreme cries from the other; and then there was no more game to it, only the rush of mind and body to the keenest, highest peak of the precipice, and the glorious plunge over its edge.

It was a very long time before they remembered that voices could also be used for speech. And it was a long, glorious summer together, but still all too short, before Hjørdis had to go back for the winter to her father's Hall by the sea. Another summer followed, and winter as well, when she took up the permanent position of Lady of her uncle's Hall, seeing to his care in his old age and to the well-being of all the people of his lands.

Styggri was healer of both trolls and men, as her mother had been before her, and came often to the Hall, but was never at ease within its walls. Hjørdis took every chance to be with her in the troll's hut, more cave than structure, where they lay wrapped together in furs or hides and the heat of their own bodies. It was never enough, and the time of parting came ever closer.

By then they had no secrets from each other. Hjørdis had known from the first that Styggri could merge her body into stones; now she knew that certain trolls, with enough instruction, had the power to travel through entire mountains. And she knew that Styggri was bound by oath and heritage to return to the great undergound Hall sacred to trollkind, and from there, after yet more years of training, to pass through walls of stone and time into a world where trolls still lived and hunted as they had ages ago, where there were great cliffs of ice, and massive long-haired creatures with trunks and curving tusks, and the elk were twice as tall as any now living. A world from which there was no return.

Hjørdis knew more surely than all else that Styggri was torn, longing to stay with her, yet eager to see the wonders of that distant world. It didn't matter. Duty and tribal bonds were inviolable.

Hjørdis did not want to be told the day of departure, so one day Styggri was simply gone. It was weeks before Hjørdis could bring herself to revisit their grotto behind the waterfall. If she shed tears when she found the polished garnet pendant left there as a gift for her, a blood-red token of their wounded hearts, she could tell herself that the dampness was merely droplets of the torrent's spray.

Now, by this bridge across a placid stream in a hostile land, Hjørdis was bound by oath and duty, while Styggri was free.

"How did you..."

"You bound me to this world after all." Their arms were tight around each other, and Styggri spoke against Hjørdis's tawny hair. "I could not pass beyond the final barrier, and at last they understood that my heart was held to this world too strongly to let me leave it. The council of wise women took it as a sign that I would be of better use remaining to care for the remnant of trollkind who must stay behind. I will travel the high places where the old ones remain, but come always home to you. Once I get you there."

Hjørdis pulled away. "You know I am bound here by oath." She did not believed for a moment that Styggri truly thought she had come here by choice.

"Then why aren't you well on the way to fulfilling it? And why you? The king has daughters, and your goat of a brother is under lock and key. What more does he need to ensure a strong grandson? Harald has sired more husky bastard sons already than he can count. Make him marry one of the girls. They seem quite obsessed with goats as it is."

"The king holds that the mother's strength is the key. His own wife was beautiful but frail. If his son cannot manage to mount me, he has made it plain that he will handle the matter himself, which, since that is not part of my bargain, would result in grievous bodily injury to him and a likely death sentence for me."

"Not while I am here," Styggri said grimly. "But if you're set on breeding with the prince, mount him yourself. I've watched their games. What that lad wants is tying up and ravishing." Her mood lightened. "I could hold him down for you."

"You would frighten him into spending his juice before I had a chance at it. Now that you've told me what I should have known myself, I'll handle it. And no, you may not watch. I would be too tempted to laugh."

There were sounds of the merrymakers returning from their sport. "I'll meet you here early in the morning while they think I still sleep. Go now!"

Styggri hesitated, then drew a packet from the pouch at her belt and nudged it into Hjørdis's hand. "Take this with your wine. For success tonight." In another instant she had melted away through the birches downstream.

That night in her bedchamber Hjørdis prepared for her husband's coming. His eyes widened when he saw her, all but naked in the most revealing of the undergarments from her wardrobe, and when he tore his gaze away from her full breasts thrusting out above tight lacing his mouth gaped wide at the sight of the willow switch she was tapping against one hand.

"Take off your clothes, boy," she said sternly.

Oh...yes! Yes, Mistress!" He fumbled at his garments, never looking away from her even when she applied the switch to his bared flanks with some force.

"Now lie back on the bed and grip the bedposts."

He complied without a word, only an occasional whimper when she flicked the switch across the most tender of his exposed parts. Tying him was clearly unnecessary, but she did it, and even though he was not tall enough for his ankles to reach the foot of the bed with his wrists bound with cords to the headposts, he writhed in place as though they too were restrained.

Slight as he was, when Hjørdis had alternately teased and switched him for a short time he was clearly tall enough where it counted. She tweaked her own breasts and envisioned Styggri's large hands on them to get her juices flowing enough for comfort, and, when his cries and gasps signaled that it would soon be too late, she mounted and rode him fiercely until he was drained and sobbing.

Hjørdis was far from drained, but she untied the prince and allowed him to sleep in her arms all night, his head nestled between her breasts. She herself slept little, dreaming of Styggri, but too fitfully for relief.

At dawn the castle was in an uproar. Hjørdis gave up any pretense of sleep, sent the prince away, and cornered her maid. The girl was longing to tell the news. Princess Vesla had been found in the prisoner's bed, and was defying her father through her tears, proclaiming that she would marry Harald or die. Some whispered that she had gone to him through a secret passage beneath the castle, but the castle was built on rock, so that must be untrue.

In the turmoil Hjørdis slipped out unseen, pausing in the laundry yard behind the stables to exchange her finery for

leggings and a shirt of suitable size. As soon as she reached the
bridge Styggri appeared among the trees.

Hjørdis confronted her, eyes blazing in anger. "A secret
passage? There was a secret passage through the rock?"

Styggri retreated a step or two and shrugged. "Well, there
is now."

"And what other useful lessons did you learn in all those
years of training? I suppose poor Vesla's wine, like mine,
contained herbs with special powers."

"Not quite the same herbs," Styggri said. "And do not pity
Princess Vesla. She had the courage to follow the counsel of
the fearsome troll who appeared in a 'dream.' She will bear a
healthy son, so if the king has the sense to get them quickly wed,
your oath will be fulfilled. Or near enough."

"I will not be managed!" Hjørdis was every inch the Lady
of the Hall. "I do not presume to command you, nor you me.
There must be no secrets between us!" Styggri, for all her solid
strength, looked shaken, until Hjørdis took her by the sleeve
and tugged her toward the rocky cleft from which the stream
flowed. "Well, what are you waiting for? We must be far away
and hidden by the time they think to search for me."

By noon they were well away to the north. Where they must
pass through open land, night travel would be best, so they
rested in a dense hillside copse above a rocky ledge through the
afternoon. Once settled in, Hjørdis sighed and leaned against
Styggri's shoulder, and when she felt a tentative arm across her
shoulders, she put her own around Styggri's waist. Was Styggri
too wondering what lay ahead for them? Each had changed in
the years apart. Yet she knew already that Styggri was her truest
home, more to her than any mountains or fjords or Halls.

There was one question left unanswered. "Why," she asked,
"since you had built your plan around Vesla, did you urge me on
to seduce Prince Oleg? Merely part of your game?"

"No game." Styggri drew a deep breath. "No game, but something that should have been your choice, not mine."

Hjørdis forged on. "'Not quite the same herbs,' you said. And now you are sure that she will bear a son."

"There was no time for discussion. But…surely there should be another Lady of your Hall to come after you…"

Hjørdis had already considered this possibility. By now her rage had been spent, replaced by a small flicker of hope. A daughter. Yes.

She shifted until her body pressed Styggri's backward. The blood-red garnet pendant slid out from beneath her shirt, dangling from its silver chain, and she swayed deliberately so that it bobbed against Styggri's lips. "Conception without benefit of pleasure? You have a great deal to make up for!"

Their bodies still knew each other as well as they knew themselves. Taste did not lie, nor scent, nor touch. Both were strong and fiery enough to wish for no gentleness; that could be savored later. Hjørdis's grip ranged over Styggri's rump and back and shoulders, leaving trails of bruises and scratches, until Styggri's hot mouth on one breast, then the other, and the skill of her agile tongue, made Hjørdis tug frantically at her head to get that mouth pressed even harder against peaks that were swollen and tender, yet ached for more and more.

Styggri, her hand as busy between Hjørdis's wet folds as her mouth on those full breasts, clamped her own thighs fiercely around the one Hjørdis raised between them, so that each movement by one, every thrust and arch of hips, every stroke of fingers, heightened the other's pleasure. The shattering peak was reached all too soon, followed, after a brief interval of catching their breaths, by new entanglements and challenges, and equal triumphs.

By the time Hjørdis had gained what she was due and more, with much rolling and wrestling and the heat of maximum friction, they were both sore, scratched by branches and each other, and supremely satisfied.

Hjørdis lay curled on her side, panting, her head on her lover's belly. "Here is the choice I make," she said at last. "If we are to raise a daughter, a child of the Hall by blood, and of Trollkind by love"—she felt Styggri's sharp intake of breath— "her name will be Magnhild, for any daughter of ours must become a strong, valiant woman."

Styggri, with a long, contented sigh, let Hjørdis have the last word, for nothing further need be said.

# THE SORCERESS
# OF SOLISTERRE

### Lea Daley

The polished torchwood table seemed to stretch to infinity. Seated at its head, Ilyaviere the Third—Queen of Solisterre, Venestria, and the Prithian Islands—counted the councillors in attendance. All present, twenty grave faces turned toward their sovereign. But aligned with one another, in opposition to her.

Conscious that too much conflict might cause the immense table to ignite, the monarch faced the prime minister and chose her words carefully. "Marriage is a weighty matter, not to be undertaken hastily, Lord Nestrington."

"Yet not to be deferred forever," he countered.

That was true. After ten years on the throne, Ilyaviere understood that certain obligations were nonnegotiable. She belonged to Solisterre, existed only for its purposes, had less freedom than any laborer. Now at five-and-twenty, the pressure to wed increased with each passing day.

The prime minister regarded his queen from beneath hooded eyes. Rumor had it she was lusty between the linens, but had never given her heart to a lover. Ilyaviere was like high summer's afternoon—resplendent, golden, fiery, seductive, flowering. Always too warm, she dressed in the gauziest of robes, threw open windows, flung off coverlets. Her intemperate heat was a perilous distraction, Nestrington thought, capable of warping sound judgment. And actively dangerous in concert with the torchwood table. "Moreover, Majesty," the prime minister said cautiously, "with Helgartha gone to Summerland, your empire is at ever greater risk."

Ilyaviere's amber eyes blazed. How dare Nestrington patronize her? Who knew better that Solisterre—so rich, so desirable—was dreadfully vulnerable to attack now? Without Helgartha's intuitive powers, her impregnable spells, enemy forces would soon be on the march. If they weren't already massing at the borders. Then Ilyaviere's subjects, young and old, would be hostage to fortune. The table grew warmer, the queen's voice cold. "I have summoned a new witch, as well you know. She is due within this week. Taliander assures me she possesses the skills necessary to safeguard our lands."

At the mention of the high priestess, Lord Nestrington changed tactics. Steepling his fingers, the prime minister spoke delicately. "There is also the matter of an heir, Majesty. Which is another form of security."

An inarguable statement. The line of succession in Solisterre stretched back some three thousand years unchallenged, every monarch blood kin to Ilyaviere. She could delay no longer. "Very well. Make the arrangements. We shall begin receiving candidates forthwith." Twenty sets of shoulders relaxed.

But twenty pairs of eyes narrowed when the queen raised a regal palm. "However, I will only accept someone who sees me truly, loves me deeply, strengthens me where I am weak, and accepts such gifts and faults as I may possess. I will marry one who venerates neither my wealth nor my position, but only my spirit—in bed and out. Find such a suitor, high-born or low, rich or poor, and I will wed."

She pressed judicious fingertips to the tabletop, which was gathering fire as her councillors fought back angry rejoinders. Rising, Ilyaviere smiled upon them. "Pray forgive me, gentlemen. I must take my leave before we induce a conflagration."

Head in his hands, the prime minister sat alone in the council hall until the gleaming table cooled. Thinking, *At least when Helgartha was alive, Solisterre had a mature presence guiding the helm—even if she was only a woman, subject to every female caprice and vagary. It's past time for a man to rule the empire again. And I know just the fellow for the task.*

Back in her chambers, the queen was far too heated to wait for assistance. Tossing the ancestral diadem to the bed, throwing off her formal garb, she asked her ladies, "Has the white witch yet arrived?"

"No, Majesty. Perhaps she is delayed by poor weather to the north."

Ilyaviere paced impatiently. "Having lost my dear Helgartha, I am in dire want of her talents." And for the first time, the queen admitted to herself how much she needed the counsel and support of another shrewd old woman, another surrogate mother. "Present her to me as quickly as may be, no matter the hour. She may dine here."

In fact, Helgartha's successor was only a witch-in-training, albeit an Estrellian adept, able to freeze time and motion at will. She had also an emergent flair for sensing trend lines, the tilt of cosmic probability, the faintest strands of interconnection. Still, Aivlynn Janisdottir seemed a peculiar choice for the Queen's Court—nay, for Her Majesty's most essential advisor—and an extremely unlikely channel for the awesome powers required of a royal sorceress. Certainly she thought herself too green to defend an ancient empire. And this was a time of great hazard. Unguarded Solisterre was the jewel of the continent, with a thousand miles of coastline, deepwater ports, mild climate, fertile fields, unparalleled craftsmen, and coffers overflowing. Wherefore Aivlynn wondered what Taliander had been thinking to anoint someone so untried. Again and again she reviewed the high priestess's parting words. "Fear not, my daughter. You are more than ready for the tests that lie ahead. You are *right* for them. And your capacities will only gain potency over time."

Yet how wrenching it had been for Aivlynn to leave the only home she remembered! The venerable Wiccan community, that small world of wise women and their aspiring acolytes. The Grandaliese Forest, where she'd spent her girlhood studying whitecraft. The sheltering stone dormitory, where the Four Rules—Live, Love, Learn, Enjoy—were carved above the entrance, and unfailingly observed within. Even now, her friends remained there, happy and carefree, unburdened by the weight of encroaching responsibility.

Despite the urgency, though, despite impending danger, Aivlynn had declined transport to Denethra—royal seat of Solisterre—choosing instead to walk the Hallowed Way. For she needed the length of that transit, needed time to ponder the mystery of her appointment. Much too soon she'd be a captive of the queen's court, imprisoned in unsought luxury by her own extraordinary aptitudes.

Each noon, she supped at some local inn. And afterward, she amused herself by playing her flute in the marketplace for an hour. Releasing a deceptively simple minor-key tune into the air, a song designed to strip passersby of pretense. Many mistook her for a busker, a few tossed coins her way—some from generosity, others for show. Aivlynn never had to guess at their motivations, for in the presence of her music, a person's true essence was revealed. She watched a scold stroll past, and a peacemaker.

A miser and a misanthrope. A meddler and an altruist. But she alone saw the secrets of their hearts.

On her last night of travel, she slept outdoors, on the generous bosom of fair Gaia, under the protection of Mother Moon. Sheltering below the downward curving branches of a kibko tree, she was little more than a shiver of loneliness concealed beneath her thick cloak, awaiting the turn of the world, the comfort of the sun. When day broke, Aivlynn made a meal of succulent kibko berries, and bathed in a nearby stream. Then she gathered her courage and pointed her feet toward Castle Paschendrale.

"Aivlynn Janisdottir!" a herald announced in stentorian tones. "Most Solemnly Anointed Sorceress to the Queen of Solis-terre, Venestria, and the Prithian Islands!" Every lord and lady pivoted toward the entrance of the grand receiving room. What they saw was winter's dawn. Frost white, crystal clear. A wisp of a woman with hair so pale it was almost ivory and eyes the changeable lavender-blue of ice caves when struck by sun. An aura of magic swirled around her, deep and chill as antediluvian wells. Healing. Nigh giddy with relief at her timely arrival, the court bowed welcome in perfect synchronicity.

Aivlynn felt she was in a dream as she walked a narrow plush carpet that seemed ten thousand leagues long. At the end, a dais. On the dais, a throne. On the throne, a queen—Ilyaviere the Third. In her presence, welcome warmth roared through Aivlynn. When the white witch rose from a deep curtsy, the women's eyes met, then locked with almost palpable shock.

*No mother figure, this!* the monarch mused, while source-less breezes cooled her. Uncommonly flustered by the sorceress's dewy youth, Ilyaviere greeted her candidly. "I'd thought you to be much older."

"*I* had thought *you* more vulnerable," Aivlynn replied, such forthrightness only permissible as her unique proficiencies near rivaled royal status.

"It pleases the council to represent me so," the queen murmured with a cynicism greatly heightened by the rigors of her role. "You come to me at a thorny time, Aivlynn Janisdottir. There is much work to be done—and undone."

When the witch closed those mesmerizing eyes, Ilyaviere could almost see tendrils of mystical power drifting outward, seeking, assessing. "Indeed," Aivlynn affirmed. "Menace lies all around you. Within and without Castle Paschendrale."

"Hopefully nothing that cannot wait till after our bonding ceremony three days hence." Gesturing toward a table laden with exotic food and drink, the queen added, "Partake of what pleases you, then rest if need be. As is customary, your chambers adjoin mine."

Ilyaviere turned her attention to a messenger, but the prime minister's gaze never left the newly appointed sorceress. *Madame Taliander must be more muddled than I imagined,* Nestrington said to himself. *This girl couldn't thwart the most basic of invasion spells. Solisterre is ripe for the picking.*

That night the queen lay in her opulent bed separated from the sorceress by the thickness of a stone wall, consumed with thoughts of the woman. Ilyaviere was bored as only those in gilded cages can be, isolated by ultimate power and consummate authority. She had unfettered access to everything except liberty, privacy, and honest exchanges of emotion. But now came bewitching Aivlynn Janisdottir, and the world was suddenly astir with possibility.

The traditional bonding ceremony between white witch and monarch was sacred, deeply intimate, permanent. Unattended, the pair traveled to a sunstruck glen far from the castle. By the light of a waning moon, Aivlynn had prepared this space: A double circle of clarith blossoms lay on pounded earth there, a pentagram of pungent herbs within. An altar at center, displaying only a tiny flute, and a beeswax candle redolent of sweet brenebane.

"Step within, oh Queen, and kneel."

Then Ilyaviere was face-to-face with the sorceress. Whose voice was indistinguishable from enchantment itself. Whose commitment was firm, whose will unbreakable. Whose spirit was light and airy, nothing like Helgartha's. Aivlynn raised a silver flute to pliant lips. In the strains of her melody, she divined all that was necessary: Ilyaviere was bright, decent, and dedicated, but impetuous. The headstrong queen would profit from a moderating partner.

Enmeshed in the mood of that music, Ilyaviere saw something new. Always she'd thought white witches eschewed evil in favor of doing good. Now she understood why Taliander had elevated Aivlynn; this woman was simply incapable of malice. She walked a path illuminated by her own internal light. No dragons awaited her command, no miraculous wand did her bidding. Her only weapons were that shining spirit and the force of hard-won whitecraft. Yet the high priestess had judged those sufficient.

"Strange are the workings of your flute," the queen observed.

"Music is naught but mathematics, which cannot lie—song is the very soul of the universe, Majesty."

"Mayhap we should keep the special properties of your instrument secret?"

"You anticipate me, Highness."

Extending a practiced hand, the witch sketched a protective rune on Ilyaviere's forehead, then others conjuring wisdom and restraint. The touch of her finger sparked deep, unnamable emotions in the young queen. Fine strands of connection grew up between the two, twining round them, an unexpected intensity startling both—for it was a physical thing, seemingly, as well as a spiritual one, their very atoms intermingling. Wholly unlike the maternal-child bond Helgartha had woven so long ago.

Arising at last, the women glided solemnly back toward the castle. And if something inside Ilyaviere longed to clasp Aivlynn's cool hand, that was unnecessary. For she was henceforth alone nevermore.

The queen and her sorceress became fast friends, their pleasure in companionship evident to all, their trust in each other absolute. Ilyaviere never doubted that Aivlynn would fearlessly confront any perceptible threat to Solisterre. Yet the witch's singular innocence equipped her poorly for anticipating the perfidy of men—a lesson every princess must learn in her nursery, or perish prematurely.

As Aivlynn went about the vital business of blanketing each hill and valley in the borderlands with impenetrable charms, the populace calmed. Every access to the realm was soon secure, though the sorceress would endlessly be engaged in the business of reevaluation. All the adjacent territories had mages almost as talented as she, and many who were far more devious. They would continuously probe for vulnerabilities, and any identified would be exploited—to Solisterre's detriment. Just outside the drawbridge, Aivlynn whispered one further defensive incantation. For the nonce, at least, anyone might leave Castle Paschendrale, but only the approved could enter.

Those included a half-dozen suitors for Ilyaviere's hand, each specifically selected by Lord Nestrington. Not one of them low born or unknown, not one poor or powerless, despite the queen's dictates. All acceptable mates for even the grandest lady, each fluent in Solistine, because, as Ilyaviere noted acerbically, "I must be able to converse with my husband!"

But one candidate was so wealthy, so virile, so powerful, the prime minister had cast his lot with that prince. Sending stealthy couriers to and fro, he signaled his allegiance—and his willingness to subjugate Ilyaviere after marriage. For Nestrington thought women poor vessels of authority. Entirely too emotional, too empathic, too apt to display weakness, wholly unsuited to matters military. Wherefore, the first courtship visits would be mere shams, notwithstanding all their pomp and circumstance. Nestrington was saving the best for last.

While the prime minister established elaborate protocols for greeting Ilyaviere's suitors, the queen devised a plan of her own. "When the gentlemen pay me court in my bedchamber, Aivlynn, you must sit behind yonder curtain, playing soft music on your flute."

The sorceress instantly grasped the queen's intent. Still, her stomach roiled and ragged breath caught in her throat. "But, Majesty..." she stammered, "I would be...privy to...events of a most personal nature."

Ilyaviere sent a captivating smile the witch's way, laid a hand on her slim arm. "There can be no secrets between queen and her most valued counselor. Without you, I would know nothing but the artful face every man presents. You will see each to his very core. Only with your aid will I identify a proper consort."

The applicants arrived at carefully spaced intervals over a period of months, six nobles from surrounding realms, all bent on marriage to Solisterre's unmatched regent. Without exception, Ilyaviere noted, they were titled and landed, wealthy in their own right. And each was handsomer and stronger than the one before. Days of sport, feasting, and dance followed their introductions into the court, until finally came nights of amorous assessment. Every aristocrat was ushered in turn to the queen's chambers.

Unseen, Aivlynn sat on a stool there, just beyond a heavy tapestry, instrument in hand. As Ilyaviere bedded her suitors, the witch's heart pounded wildly and her mind was abuzz with unthinkable longings. First came Finnid the Seventh, Baron of South Mervaglia, a sprawling agricultural region that produced exceptional wines and had historic trading ties with Solisterre. Aivlynn rested her flute against trembling lips, hoping her fey melody would block all sound emanating from the other side of the tapestry. A fall of satin slithering to the floor. The baron's confident laughter. A rhythmic escalation of breath. The distinctive sound of flesh on flesh. For hearing the slightest hint of excitement in the queen's voice filled Aivlynn with inexplicable despair.

In seconds, the sorceress knew Finnid was not the mate for Ilyaviere. For the next hour, then, she could simply play her songs without summoning supernatural forces. And as Aivlynn fingered the silver keys, she focused her total attention on the antique tapestry, counting the minuscule stitches on its reverse, comparing its fading colors to nature, wondering why she felt so disconsolate. At last her dismal obligation ended. In the morning, she would break bread with the queen, hoping her report found favor, not knowing what would transpire if they were at odds with one another.

"What say you of Finnid?" Ilyaviere inquired, smoothing a napkin over her lap.

The sorceress studied those dancing eyes, then looked deeper, seeking insight from her sovereign's psyche. Reassured to sense they were in accord, she answered, "The man is a hopeless egotist."

"Born and bred." Ilyaviere laughed. "At table, the baron spoke only of his own appetites. And in bed—"

"It was no different?"

"It is as you surmise, my friend. Once he was sated himself, he assumed he'd pleasured me."

Despite the queen's frustration, something inside Aivlynn

leaped with joy. "Yet," she remarked, "it appears that you parted with the gentleman on good terms."

Ilyaviere nodded. "While dancing, we agreed to a most beneficial exchange. For the privilege of grazing Mervaglian livestock on underutilized fields within my domain, Finnid will supply our court with fine wines."

After council that day, the queen would raise the same question to her prime minister: "What think you of Baron Finnid, my lord?"

Shaking his head definitively, Nestrington made a show of contrition. "A grave disappointment, Majesty—he was not as I'd supposed. You have my sincerest apologies. Perhaps our next guest will be more suitable."

A fortnight later, Count Jovange of Withriland shared Ilyaviere's bed with equally unsatisfactory results romantic. Over a sumptuous breakfast the next day, the queen leaned toward Aivlynn, mischief in her smile. "Let me guess what the flute revealed, dear witch... Count Jovange is nothing but an ass—dismissive of my lineage, too pompous to acknowledge any other's intrinsic worth."

"You mimic my instrument excellently well, oh Queen."

"Nevertheless," Ilyaviere confided, "Jovange and I came to agreement on a matter of great significance. Withriland is fortunate to have numerous magicians well-versed at transmutation, while Solisterre's wizards are most proficient in matters of healing and augmentation. We have pledged to share knowledge that both countries may profit. We shall build an academy for that purpose. "

"An international school of magic?" Aivlynn asked, her voice rising with excitement, hoping she might one day lecture there.

"Just so. Situated right here in Denethra."

Next Ilyaviere welcomed Duke Xenobold of Renfortig to her realm. But after a night in his arms, she wailed, "What a despicable toady! He's far too fawning, too reverent of my position. I could never bear him in my presence—his submissiveness would drive me wild!"

Aivlynn grinned, while steeling herself, for there was more. Something that must be said, even if it discomfited her ruler. "Xenobold's subservience would also bring out the worst in Your Highness—and might prove lethal to his health at a time when political intrigue runs rampant."

Ilyaviere ceased spreading yanil jam to look sharply at her witch. Aivlynn met that haughty inspection without flinching. Finally the queen laughed. "How refreshing to hear the truth for once. I must send something really splendid to Taliander, in thanks for anointing you!"

After breaking her fast, the queen chanced to cross paths with Nestrington in the gardens. "How did you regard Duke Xenobold, my lord?"

The prime minister waved a flippant hand. "His reputation is greatly overstated. No doubt we can make a better match for Your Majesty."

To all appearances the sixth applicant, their neighbor to the West, was an ideal partner for Ilyaviere. For the first time, the prime minister appeared to feel that a suitor satisfied his every expectation. Prince Zanderson was heir to Underliste, a mountainous land rich in essential ores. He was somewhat older than Solisterre's queen, but not too old. Tall and muscular, with sun-browned skin, Zanderson had the requisite chiseled features, square jaw and cleft chin. His thick hair had gone appealingly silver long before its time, and his manners in court, at table, were impeccable. But for all his royal blood, for all his polish and sophistication, the prince made Aivlynn's skin crawl.

As she seated herself behind the tapestry on that fateful night, the witch wondered why this task grew harder each time. *By now*, she thought, *I should be inured to my duty. For*

*Ilyaviere must marry, and she is wise to seek my guidance, prudent to insist on testing each suitor.* Still, Aivlynn squirmed on her small stool, fighting foreign demons. The prime directive of Wicca was clear and unyielding: harm none. So why had she found within herself an urge to injure those men who so freely fondled the queen?

She struggled mightily to ignore the hallmarks of Zanderson's courtship. The masculine rumble of that princely baritone. The sound of bedclothes flung back. Muffled groans from Ilyaviere, giving way to a most exuberant form of amorous exercise. Chairs were tumbling, it seemed. Curtains rending. Precious objects crashing from mantel to floor. Shoving bewilderment aside, Aivlynn lifted her magical instrument.

The flute rendered its verdict just as the first blow landed, right before Ilyaviere shrieked in pain and outrage: Zanderson was a brute who believed that to rule was to force, to punish. He mistook women—even queens—for playthings to bend to his will. Dashing into the bedchamber, the witch tripped over splintered furniture, skidded on broken fine goods littering the marble tiles.

While Aivlynn had sat slumped in selfish gloom, her queen had fought a bitter battle. Naked now, Ilyaviere was bent over the victor's lap, both wrists restrained by an outsized hand, red welts rising on her royal rear, a whip descending. Aivlynn's response was instinctual—unchecked Estrellian magic surged through the room. Time ceased. Motion stopped. Silence fell. Caught in the grip of unearthly cold, Prince Zanderson was helpless and terror-stricken.

Releasing Ilyaviere, Aivlynn covered the queen's nakedness, led her to a chair, and lowered her onto a swansdown cushion. Then, indigo eyes glittering with glacial intensity, the witch turned to the spellbound suitor, contemplating a myriad of possibilities. Discarding, considering again.

Suddenly, the proud prince was shrinking. Squealing. Bristling with gray fur and spiky whiskers. A fat and greedy rat then, waving a wormlike tail, balancing a miniature golden crown on his wicked head, sniffing the air frantically. Leaping off that ornate chair, the creature darted from corner to corner, seeking escape. "Run, rat, run!" Aivlynn cried. "No harm will befall you between here and the outskirts of your kingdom—and there shall you revert to human form. But beyond the confines of your lands, you will forever be seen for the vermin you are!"

Wincing, Ilyaviere shifted position, bent to pluck the tiny coronet from the rat's head. A souvenir, she thought, small enough to slip on her smallest finger. A reminder of lessons learned about the risks of courtship and betrothal for women of every station. But the witch deflected her. "To stay their hands at the approach of this nasty rat, Zanderson's border guards must see the ancestral crown."

The queen sank back on that cushion, yelping at the damage done to her exalted person. "Did you speak the truth, Aivlynn? Will he never again be free to leave Underliste?"

"Never," the witch confirmed. "Also," she added, a luscious smile playing at the corners of her mouth, "I have blessed yon suitor, as well as cursing him."

"How so?"

"I have conferred exceptionally long life upon Zanderson—"

Ilyaviere's elegant eyebrows shot skyward when she deduced the political implications of that endowment. "Solisterre will be safe from Western assault for decades to come!"

"Most certainly the prince cannot lead troops against you."

The queen's face fell. "But suppose in his rage and humiliation, Zanderson sends his wizards and generals to attack us? Why should he not direct his battalions from afar?"

"Other than that he would appear a base coward? Perchance,

Majesty, you might forestall military action through diplomatic interventions of the type you craft so well."

"Ah!" Ilyaviere crowed. "We shall paint a pretty face on the matter. Possibly offer Underliste deeply advantageous trade agreements? Conceivably enter into joint defensive treaties?"

"Excellent ideas. And..."

"Yes?"

"It may be well to float a tale or two about Your Highness. That you were not so beautiful as the gentleman expected? Not as...accomplished...in bed? Mayhap a rumor that you are—forgive me—likely infertile?"

Ilyaviere clapped her hands. "Brilliant, Aivlynn! That should also discourage interest from other dreary suitors. Perhaps I shall have peace after all!"

The witch rested her hand upon the latch to the chamber door. "Have you listened well, Prince Rat? Then be gone!" And she shooed Zanderson into the hallway, closing the heavy portal behind him, laughing softly.

"What amuses you, dear witch? Beyond reducing that beast to his primal form?"

Aivlynn turned to the monarch, bowing slightly. "I have placed other significant constraints upon that knave, which shall be revealed to him in due time."

"Tell me," Ilyaviere coaxed, her face alight with curiosity.

"No longer can he lift a hand in anger—*or* erect a certain *other* appendage, whether in fair mood or foul. For the rest of his many days, no maid needs fear for her safety in Prince Zanderson's presence."

But despite Ilyaviere's radiant smile, Aivlynn sensed the queen's unabated pain—a flight of frenzied doves beating within her. "Your Highness," she stuttered, "I...I...should like to perform a healing, but..."

"To do so, you must lay hands upon my wounds."

"Truth," the sorceress acknowledged, near to fainting, awaiting instruction.

When Ilyaviere dropped that robe, the witch was struck speechless by her queen's rare beauty. Peach-velvet skin, subtle lines, with curves and planes as beautiful as anything nature ever devised. Flawless—except for the brutal marks left by a dark prince. Aivlynn marveled at the intense flood of desire washing through her, racing downstream toward treacherous falls, sweeping away all denial. How was it that she'd known everyone's heart but her own? At last, she summoned restraint, swallowed hard, and said, "Pray recline on your stomach."

Yet as Ilyaviere lay before her, that glorious mane tumbling about smooth shoulders, that sweet, tormented derriere on full display, the sorceress felt control flee. "Majesty," she murmured, astounded by her own effrontery, "I fear if I touch you, I will be unable to stop."

Brushing tawny hair from her eyes, Ilyaviere spoke in a deep, smoky voice. "I believe you may master more than *one* form of medicine before this night is through, darling witch. I command you: work your magic upon me."

At first there was only the sibilance of whispered spells—or, perhaps, endearments. Followed by the blessed relief of cool hands on stinging flesh, stroking, soothing, restorative. Next sizzling kisses at the nape of the queen's neck, warm breath at one sculpted ear. A delicate dance of fingers began then, trailing down regal thighs, and up again, dipping into beckoning mystery. Ilyaviere moaned, turned, reached for Aivlynn. Who paused scarcely a moment before leaning forward to kiss each lush and yearning breast, who brushed a thumb through silky curls at the junction of ardor and ecstasy. Whose hands, lips, tongue seemed to know exactly what was required of them.

While arching and writhing, Ilyaviere still managed to gasp, "*You*, my love! I must behold *you*! Now!"

At that, the witch worked a divestment spell. Instantly nude herself, Aivlynn basked in the queen's adoration. "Lie with me—atop me!" Ilyaviere demanded.

"Your Majesty's obedient servant," the sorceress breathed. She lowered her body onto the bed. Slipped one knee between slender thighs. Tweaked a royal nipple. Quivered as Ilyaviere rose against her over and over, crying, "What sorcery is this, witch? What spell have you cast?"

"None, Highnness, I swear. Only sincerity. Only love."

Then Aivlynn felt the touch of a trueborn queen, sure and dominant. As ever, when fire strikes ice, melting ensued—and stopped not throughout that infinite night. In each other's embrace, the lovers discovered the full spectrum of joy, from lightest caress to holiest of sensations.

At dawn, her thirst finally slaked, Ilyaviere lay in Aivlynn's arms. Blissfully cool, she realized she'd long been seeking a moon to light her darkest corners. *Here*, she thought drowsily, *is one who sees me truly yet loves me deeply. She'll strengthen me where I'm weak, accept such gifts and faults as are mine. This witch will venerate nothing but my spirit—in bed and out.*

And though Aivlynn had resided amongst women all her days, never had she guessed they held the key to her happiness. Still aflame with feverish passion—warm at last—she saw she'd always longed for a sun to orbit. But this sun was nigh to dying out. "Flare again, bright star," she urged, nuzzling a soft breast, sparking a heavenly inferno within her queen, intensifying the fire at her own core. Together then they burned through every foolish inhibition, turned every dull convention to ephemeral ash.

Resting alongside Ilyaviere as the sky lightened, the sorceress thought simply, *This is why I was sent to Castle Paschendrale. Here lies my destiny.*

\* \* \*

In council that noon, the prime minister folded his hands on the torchwood table. Noting no vestige of heat, he said suavely, "I missed Prince Zanderson in court this morning, Your Majesty. Will he dine with us this eve?"

Ilyaviere's smile was one he'd never seen before. In a voice like sun-warmed honey, she replied, "Last night in my bedchamber, Nestrington, our guest had a truly transformative experience." Across the table, men's eyes met, their randy speculations generating a hint of warming embers in the wood. "Unfortunately," Ilyaviere continued, "urgent business has called Zanderson home. Permanently."

Lord Nestrington was uncharacteristically befuddled. "Permanently? But…but…he seemed so fine a match for Your Highness!" *And I had an understanding with that scoundrel!* The prime minister's mind raced, his hands shook. *Hath anyone else knowledge of our private negotiations? Will Zanderson expose me as a traitor?*

The queen smiled that secret smile again. "He most assuredly will not return." Then she glanced at the thick sheet of parchment lying before Nestrington. "What weighs most heavily upon us this day?"

Clearing his throat, the prime minister made a visible effort to relax his furrowed brow. "The treasurer proposes recoinage—"

"Replacing my father's image on Solistine currency? Only a decade since his death?"

Nestrington bowed deferentially. "With a likeness of your faultless profile, Majesty."

"An unnecessary expense, my lord. I am not yet that vain. What else?"

"The navy seeks funding for additional warships. And"—the prime minister ventured—"I suppose, the question of a royal union remains unanswered?"

"Our armada is quite sufficient at this time, sir. As for the matter of marriage, fear not. I have that well in hand."

Ilyaviere allowed six months to spin out in thrilling courtship before proposing to Aivlynn, who was dazzled by that invitation to wed. Then overjoyed. Then doubtful. "But, Majesty...women betrothed to one another? How shall this be?"

"Do I not possess the power to define and authorize marriage as I deem fit, sweet Aivlynn? And I see no harm in Solistine ladies loving one another. Nor for that matter, our gentlemen pairing similarly. Therefore, I choose you most happily for my Queen Consort, for my constant partner in both domesticity and regency. And with your calming presence in council meetings, what need for a torchwood table to enforce civility?"

For one second, Aivlynn allowed herself the fantasy. To live, to work, to die within the circle of Ilyaviere's love? That was her heart's desire! Yet it was not feasible. "There is the troubling matter of an heir, Majesty..."

Her queen's smile was teasing, beguiling. "Is your magic truly so impotent, my love?"

Indigo eyes widened, then slowly closed, as Aivlynn sought answers to questions never before asked. Lost to Ilyaviere just then, she was adrift in a world of archaic chants, sacred spells, untapped possibility. Certain flowers filled her mind, aromatic herbs clamored for her attention. But the enchantments for quickening and fruition would be something new under the sun, something of her own devising. And blood must play a part in the elixir, a few drops from each. Drawn at first light of dawn, melded then, inseparable...

Remonstrate though he might, Nestrington could not dissuade his monarch from marriage to that damnable sorceress. Nor could he provoke opposition to her outlandish plan. Every cautious hint was heartily rejected. For the lord high admiral had overcome anger about limitations to the fleet when Aivlynn divined the whereabouts of his eldest son, gone missing on a hunting trip. The royal treasurer was deeply indebted to the white witch, whose invigorating potion had equipped him for delighting his wife once more. Lord Lethwith had been cured of debilitating insomnia, while Lord Quissic had not forgotten Aivlynn's magical healing of his favored mount. And so it went. None of the councillors Nestrington surveyed would back a scheme to deflect Queen Ilyaviere from her reckless course. The others he dared not even approach.

Wedding banns were posted throughout the empire and no citizen protested the joining of monarch with mage. On the grand day, Castle Paschendrale was hung with pennants from postern to pinnacle. Its halls were decked with garlands and cloth of gold. The streets were lined with teeming grand-stands. Scents both sweet and savory filled the air as bakers and butchers prepared for feasting. Bonfires lay ready to brighten the night. Fireworks were primed to tint Solistine skies with celebratory starbursts.

At the appointed hour, a contingent of the royal guard stood opposite one another on the drawbridge, crossing sabers overhead. When Ilyaviere stepped beneath that arch, Aivlynn was at her side. The prime minister strode close behind, his every ambition in disarray. They had not gone five paces when Nestrington's desperate voice rang forth, drowning out lute and viol. "Seize them, men! The queen, that wretched witch! Seize them!"

Before the baffled soldiers could respond, Ilyaviere was a whirling column of ire, of fire. Whipping a ceremonial dagger from her sash. Feinting. Forcing Nestrington to his knees. Challenging the guard to react. But none could, for Aivlynn had summoned howling Northalien winds, freezing all in place for a timeless interlude. Plucking out her flute, she walked the long aisle, playing a questing melody, sorting traitor from true. Freeing only those loyal to the queen. Most vile of all was Nestrington, whose heart seethed with hatred and resentment. Turned now to stone, frost creeping over him from head to toe, his face was a changeless mask of horror.

Lifting her own voice, Ilyaviere gestured toward twin rows of living statues. "Let these conspirators stand outside our gates, forevermore a deterrent to all who approach Castle Paschendrale with treachery in mind!" Turning then to Aivlynn, she said quietly, "Pray let us continue onward."

They exited the military gauntlet, passed the cheering throngs, climbed ranks of marble stairs, and knelt in a bridal bower, where they exchanged eternal pledges before Taliander, the beaming high priestess. When they sealed their vows with a kiss, unbounded revelry claimed the crowd, and their dancing lasted long past dawn.

Two years later, a princess was born of Ilyaviere. Aivlynn gazed worshipfully at tiny Ilyalynn napping in the queen's arms. "Well done, my love! Our babe is near as fair as her mother."

Joy lit Ilyaviere's eyes. "Not so, Aivlynn! She is more beautiful by far. For she looks exactly like you—another white witch, methinks."

And from first breath, all saw that Ilyalynn blended the best of both parents. In her, the chill rationality of winter had combined with the simmering passions of summer, forming a child of springtime—most temperate of seasons. A queen in the making, possessed of angelic beauty and incomparable charm, who would grow to be more leader than ruler. Wiser, kinder, more righteous than any before her. The enduring glory of Solisterre, Venestria, and the Prithian Islands.

# ABOUT THE AUTHORS

**M. BIRDS** (mbirds.tumblr.com) is a glam femme writer and filmmaker living in Vancouver, British Columbia. Her stories have been published by Freaky Fountain and Hot Ink Press. She likes witches and princesses and red wine, if you're buying.

**EMILY L. BYRNE** (writeremilylbyrne.blogspot.com) lives in lovely Minneapolis with her wife and the two cats that own them. She toils in corporate IT when not writing. She has stories in *Forbidden Fruit: Unwise Stories of Lesbian Desire* and *The Mammoth Book of Uniform Erotica.*

**LEA DALEY** wrote fiction while raising children, claiming a lesbian identity, earning a BFA, teaching, and heading a nonprofit agency. She now writes full-time. Daley's debut novel, *Waiting for Harper Lee,* received an Alice B. Lavender Certificate and was short-listed at the Golden Crown Awards. In 2015, her second book, *FutureDyke,* won a Goldie and was a Lambda finalist.

**A. D. R. FORTE** (facebook.com/ADRForte) writes a variety of short fiction for adults. Her fantasy, erotica, and erotic fantasy appear in various anthology collections.

**H. N. JANZEN** (hilary.n.janzen@gmail.com) is a Canadian writer who typically does her best work when she's supposed to be doing something else. Her favorite mythical creature is the succubus.

**MICHAEL M. JONES** (michaelmjones.com) appears in numerous publications, including *Girl Fever, A Princess Bound,* and *Bedded Bliss* (Cleis Press), and edited *Like Fortune's Fool* and *Like a Cunning Plan* (Circlet Press). He lives in Virginia with a pride of cats, and a wife who helps him make up his mind.

**ANNABETH LEONG** (annabetherotica.com) wears high heels and frequents the former haunts of H. P. Lovecraft. She is frequently confused about her sexuality, but enjoys searching for answers. Her work has appeared in *Girl Crush, Women With Handcuffs,* and many more. Her latest erotic novel is *Untouched,* from Sweetmeats Press.

**CARA PATTERSON** is an Edinburgh-based Scottish writer. She has been telling stories since before she can remember, and progressed on to writing them down as soon as she had a grasp of the alphabet. She's delighted to be able to say she is now a published author.

**MADELEINE SHADE** (shadyladyfairytales.com) writes erotic fairy tales and cross-pollinated mythic fiction drawn from her extensive studies in folklore and mythology. In addition to her steamy short stories, she is also the author of the interconnected novellas in the Shady Lady Fairy Tales series.

**SALOME WILDE** (salandtalerotica.com) has published dozens of erotic stories across the orientation spectrum, in genres from hard-boiled/noir to kaiju exotica. She is editor of *Shakespearotica: Queering the Bard* and *Desire Behind Bars: Lesbian Prison Erotica* (Bella Books), with coauthor Talon Rihai.

**BREY WILLOWS** (breywillows.com) grew up in Southern California and now lives in England. She is the author of the *Afterlife, Inc* series and enjoys writing erotica in her spare time. She's an editor and writing instructor and loves pretty much anything to do with words.

**ALLISON WONDERLAND** (aisforallison.blogspot.com) loves to kiss the girl, especially one worth fighting—and writing—for. This Sapphic storyteller's lesbian literature appears in a plethora of prurient publications, including *Girl Fever*, *Summer Love*, and *Wild Girls, Wild Nights*.

# ABOUT
# THE EDITOR

**SACCHI GREEN** (sacchi-green.blogspot.com) is a Lambda Award–winning writer and editor of erotica and other stimulating genres. Her stories have appeared in scores of publications, including eight volumes of *Best Lesbian Erotica*, four of *Best Women's Erotica*, and four of *Best Lesbian Romance*. In recent years she's taken to wielding the editorial whip, editing ten lesbian erotica anthologies, most recently *Lesbian Cowboys* (winner of a Lambda Literary Award); *Girl Crazy; Lesbian Lust; Women with Handcuffs; Girl Fever; Wild Girls, Wild Nights* (also a Lambda Award Winner); and *Me and My Boi*, all from Cleis Press. Sacchi lives in the Five College area of western Massachusetts.